MY BESTIES 3

The Downfall

Asia Hill

GOOD 2 GO PUBLISHING

ISBN: 978-1-943686-78-0
Copyright ©2015
Published 2015 by Good2Go Publishing
7311 W. Glass Lane • Laveen, AZ 85339
www.good2gopublishing.com
twitter @good2gobooks
G2G@good2gopublishing.com
Facebook.com/good2gopublishing
ThirdLane Marketing: Brian James
Brian@good2gopublishing.com
Cover design: Davida Baldwin
Interior Layout: Mychea, Inc

Printed in the U.S.A.

Acknowledgements

I thank Allah for blessing me with the talent to write.

To my three J's: Jae'lyn, Ja'taya, and Jacob. Thank you for the unconditional love that you continue to show me. I love you forever and always.

A special thank you to Ms. Detra Young. Thank you for believing in my work and in me. I appreciate you greatly!

To my readers, I try to give you my all in every book. Thank you for giving me a chance.

To my amazing and wonderful fiancé, Lindell. We had each other when the outside world turned their back on us. You are my forever man, and I can't wait to be your wife. Thank you for the love and support you continue to show me every day. You helped make me a better person. 'Til death ... and beyond!

Prison wasn't just a punishment for me. It was my second chance. I encourage everybody out there and behind these walls to go for what you want. Never use your situation as an excuse. There are no limitations when it comes to what you want. The only thing stopping you is you.

Albert Hill, Sr. ... There's not a day that goes by that I'm not thinking of you. I miss you so much, Granddaddy!

To my most trusted pen pal, Ms. Mary Tucker. Granny, thank you for being here for me. Your letters mean the world to me. I love you, my favorite girl. I can't wait to taste that good ole peach cobbler.

Good2Go, we got another one!

MY BESTIES 3

The Downfall

Prologue

How didn't I see this coming? I didn't want to go like this. I was only 16 years old, but I had been fighting all my life. I fought to be loved. I fought for respect. I fought for everything. Shit, I was tired. Now was the time that I really needed to fight. I didn't think I had it in me anymore. I began feeling light-headed. What a fucked up way to go!

ONE

Chapter

Boo

"Jaw, I know what the fuck I just said. Since you are acting slowly, let me say it again. The police just came and took JuJu. They said she was being charged with the murders of Tamiko St. Clair and that bitch, Tae."

"What the fuck? I saw all of them police outside. Poohman and I dipped after we put Tiki's mother out. Where do you think they took her?"

"I don't know, but that ain't even the half. I was on the phone with Lil Mama telling her what happened when I heard her scream my name. After that, the phone went dead. Jaw, I need to find my sister. Check the police stations. They're not supposed to question her without an adult since she's a minor."

"I got you, Auntie. Go find Lil Mama. I got JuJu."

I called around to every hospital in the area. Finally, after hours of searching, I found out that she had been taken to Holy Christ. If they take you to Christ, it's serious. Fuck serious – near death is more like it. I said a small prayer before I went inside the hospital. For some reason, I had an eerie feeling as I approached the receptions desk.

"Excuse me, can you please tell me if Aja Hills was recently brought in?"

"Who are you to Ms. Hills?"

"I'm her sister."

"Okay, hold on."

She typed something on her keyboard, paused, and then gave me the saddest look ever. My heart broke into a million pieces.

"Please don't look at me like that."

"I don't know, just come with me."

She led me through a series of doors into the emergency room. The air was so thick with death that I wanted to puke. We walked to the last exam room. She looked at me and pulled the curtain back. What I saw next made me scream like a wounded animal. "OH GOD ... NOOOOO!"

Jaw

I called precinct after precinct trying to find my girl. Double murder? Damn, that shit had me sick to my stomach.

I couldn't imagine my baby going to prison for that shit. Why would the police even assume it was her? Something wasn't right. I needed to get in touch with Tiki's girlfriend. She was working in the district that the murders happened in.

"Poohman, you know where I could get Tiki's girl number from?"

"Let me hit ReRe. I know she's got it."

My phone began to ring. I saw 'private' on the screen.

"Who the fuck is this? Hello? Who is this?"

"Who I am is not important. What I have to say might help ya, girl."

"Okay, I'm listening."

"Lil Man called Crime Stoppers and blamed JuJu for them double murders."

"Who is this man?"

"Stop asking questions. I just told you why the police took your girl. Now you have to do something for me."

"How am I gonna do that when I don't even know who you are."

"Cute. I got your number. When it's time, I'll call you back."

I hung up the phone, and Poohman was looking at me as if I was crazy.

"Nigga what?"

"Who the fuck was that?"

"Some hoe that told me Lil Man called Crime Stoppers and told them that Ju was responsible for them murders."

"And the crazy part about that is if they fingerprint the crib, they gonna find her prints all over that motha fucka. Damn Joe, that's fucked up."

"Man, Poohman, we've got to find that nigga. I'm a blow his ass to pieces. We can't let her rot in jail behind that shit man."

"She's not, nigga. We gon' find out where he stay, don't trip."

Lil Man

After watching the police take JuJu into custody, I began to feel content. Two down and two more to go. Now I had to properly plan my next move. I was now going after Dirty and ReRe. I knew that after killing Tiki and sending JuJu to jail, those other two bitches were going to be on full alert. I was going to have to stay low-key because I knew that young Meech was coming after me.

I don't give a fuck about dying. I just want to make those hoes pay for what they did before I go. After running the streets all day, it was time for me to lay it down for a while. I parked my stolen car like three blocks from the crib that I was staying at. You could never be too careful around this bitch. I was a wanted man. Damn that's crazy. I wasn't even 15 yet. Doubted that I was even gon' make it there. I was gonna raise as much hell as I could before they lay me in the dirt. I walked through the alley between Burnham and Muskegon. I been laying low at JoJo's sister Mia's. I didn't feel right staying there because I really didn't trust them hoes. I was stuck because at that moment I had nowhere else to go. If I think that they're on some funny shit, I'm gonna kill 'em both. Simple as that! I prefer sneaking into the crib to catch them off guard. I slowly crept through the back door into the kitchen and saw JoJo sleeping on the couch in the living room. I heard a noise coming from the bathroom, so I pulled out my gun. I was too paranoid for this shit. I put my ear up to the door and listened. It was Mia in the bathroom. Who is she talking to?

"Stop asking questions. I just told you why the police took your girl. Now you have to do something for me."

What the fuck? Seriously, who the fuck was she talking too? I continued on listening.

"Cute. I got your number. When it's time, I'll call you back.

Yeah okay, bitch. Whatever you're up to, I'm going to find out. I heard the door lock click, so I turned around, took three large steps into the living room, and turned back around, as if I was coming from the front of the house. Mia came out of the bathroom and went to the refrigerator.

"What's cracking, Mia?"

I guess I must have scared the shit outta her, because she damn near jumped outta her skin.

"Boy you scared the hell out of me. Why you sneaking up on me like that?"

"I ain't sneak up shit. I walked up. What you up to these days?"

"Shit, still moving dat dough. Nothing else really matters. You a'ight?"

"I'm good. Just trying to figure a few things out. I really appreciate you letting me stay here. I feel like family."

She turned her head back to what she was doing and then spoke. "JoJo told me your situation. You are family now. Just don't be tryin' fuck all in my house. Y'all too young for all that."

"Yeah I got you. Can I see your phone to check on my lil sister? My phone is dead."

Dirty E

I've been walking around this bitch in my own little world. I just lost two of my bitches back-to-back. One to the grave and one to jail. When the police grabbed Ju, I thought we were all going to go. I was scared as hell. We had done so much crazy shit; I thought that Re and I were going too. When I found out what she was charged with, my whole world felt as if it was crumbling down. The shit was all-bad. We did our *thang* taking over. We had everything under control. To be real with y'all, shit didn't start going bad until Tiki's lil bro came around. Lil Man was able to get the drop on us. That nigga did some serious damage. He killed Ju's cousin, Ty. I returned the love by whacking that nigga's mama. Somehow, he gained the upper hand on us because he killed Meech and Tiki's auntie. He got Tiki that same night.

We took a major loss with that one. He wasn't the only one to blame; I blame myself as well. I should have killed that nigga at the bank. Instead, I asked Meech to do it, but he didn't. I also should have killed that bitch JoJo. I didn't know that she was Big Moe's cousin. Had Tiki not heard a conversation that JoJo was having with Lil Man, I could have easily been in Tiki's place. ReRe and I are going to get to the bottom of this shit. Unfortunately for JuJu, neither of us are adults. I can't go check on her at the station, but I know who can.

TWO

Chapter

JuJu

I still can't believe this shit. How in the world could I be
charged with two murders? That doesn't make sense. All the
police told me was that if I didn't cooperate with them that I'd
spend the rest of my life in jail with a bitch named Big Bertha.
The ride to the station took forever. We got on the expressway,
then back off of it, drove through the side streets, and then back
onto the expressway once more. If I didn't know any better, I
would have sworn that they were trying to confuse me as to where
they were taking me. I just shook my head. I was young, but T
was far from dumb. One of the officers continually looked back at
me.

"What are you looking at?"

"You! How did you get yourself mixed up into all of this
mess?"

"What mess? I haven't done shit."

"Oh, so you think you're tough? We'll see who's tough when
you go down for double murder."

"I didn't kill nobody. Tamiko was my best friend. I would

have died for her."

"Well what about the other one?"

"What about her?"

"You don't seem too sad about her."

"Would you if she treated you like shit your entire life? I don't care to discuss her. As a matter fact, I'm done talking to you, Officer Friendly. I want my lawyer."

The officer laughed as if I said something funny. "Good luck Ms. Tough Ass!"

Officer Dixon

These last few days have been unusually hard on me. I lost my girlfriend, my baby, my heart. Tiki was like a breath of fresh air. Her slick ass lied about her age when we first met. I had no idea she was only 16. She was so mature. I can't believe that she's gone. I also can't believe that they charged her best friend with the murder. That shit didn't sit right with me at all. JuJu would never harm her. There's so much shit going on, and I am dead smack in the middle of it. My partner was as shady as they came. And to make matters worse, our supervisor was his mentor. This is where it all got messy. My ex-partner House, aka 'A', was a dangerous man. I snuck in Malone's office one day when he and A were on a call. For some reason, House's file was sealed. Apparently back in the late '80s, he was a big-time drug dealer and gang member. He got into a lot of trouble and decided that he was going to work with the Feds. Ole suck ass nigga. The Feds let him do whatever he wanted to do as long as he told on his competition. After having everybody around him locked up, he decided that he wanted to do something different. I guess reality must have set in. The people that he put away weren't going to be gone for life. He was from the streets. He knew better. Those niggas was coming home to get his ass. He somehow convinced Malone to help him join the police force. Nobody in their right mind was going to come home and try to kill a cop. He gave a new definition to dirty cop. When he asked me to work the case operation "Take Down," I didn't hesitate. I wanted some action in my life. I never intended to fall for one of our suspects. It was luck that I even ran across her. Putting my badge and life on the line, I got involved with Tiki's business. I just wanted to keep her safe. After learning that my partner shot Boo and she didn't die, I knew that shit was about to hit the fan. My partner had it out for Boo and the E.S.C. Not to mention, Tiki and her besties stole over $350,000 from three very dangerous people. Apparently, House and his street informant Pancho had planned to use the girls to rob the garage. After that, Pancho was supposed to kill them. Underestimating the girls cost Pancho his life. House was livid. He was going to stop at nothing until he killed my girl and her friends, plus Boo. I had to kill him. Had I not, he would have surely brought me down with him. Now with House gone, Malone was suspicious. I think I was on his list of suspects. *ring ring*

"Officer Dixon, How can I help you?"

"Malone wants you in his office AS SOON AS POSSIBLE!"

"Okay, I'm on my way."

I already had my story together. I mean, what could really go wrong? Let me not say that, because dealing with dirty cops, everything can go wrong. I arrived at the precinct in no time. Walking towards Malone's office, I felt so sure of myself. I mean, I was really careful when I snuck into House's building. *knock knock*

"Come in."

"You wanted to see me, sir?"

"Yes, Officer Dixon. Have a seat. How ya holding up?"

"I'm trying to process all of this. Losing a partner is hard, I really liked House."

"If you really liked him, why the fuck did you kill him?"

"WHAT? I didn't shoot House! Why would you think that?"

I almost shat myself. Who the fuck has he been talking to? Damn, I'm going to jail. Trying to keep my composure, I stared him down. After what felt like hours, he smiled.

"Just kidding, Dixon. Lighten up, will ya? You're so tense."

"Boss, don't play with me like that. That shit ain't funny."

"You're right, it's not. Tell me what happened on your account."

"House texted me and told me to meet him at his house after 12. He said we had something to dispose of. When I got to his apartment I found him and Blake DOA."

"Something ain't right. Let me ask you something."

"Sure."

"Did House share any information about him making a little extra money on the side?"

Something in my head told me, *'Bitch, you better lie. Don't tell him the truth.'*

"No sir. I never even knew he made anything extra on the side."

"We have a suspect in that double homicide on 88th and Marquette. I got a tip from Crime Stoppers. I managed to convince the judge to sign off on a warrant."

My blood began to boil. You dirty piece of shit. You can't just get a warrant like that without evidence. One tip ain't enough to do that. I was real curious to know how he got the judge to sign off on that warrant.

"Well, who did you arrest?"

"One of them E.S.C. bitches. I believe her name is Ja'ziya Campbell."

It killed me to have to play along with him. I had already known that JuJu was arrested.

"Let me question her since House and I were on that operation takedown case."

"No! It really don't matter what she says. Her ass is going down for the murders."

"Why put that on her if she didn't do it? Boss, I thought that we as officers protect and serve."

"First off, who the fuck do you think you are to question me? I didn't know that you were Ms. Do the Right Fucking Thing! The mayor is on my ass again for the increase of crime going on in that area. They found her fingerprints all over the crime scene. That spells guilty in my book."

Poor baby had to do something.

"Okay, you're the boss."

"Damn right I am. We're done here. I.A. will be calling for you soon in regards to what you saw at House's place. You can go."

No sooner that I closed the door and my phone rang.

"Hello? Who is this?"

"Ash? This E. Can you talk?"

"E, it's all bad for JuJu. She's here at the station. Y'all better get her a lawyer AS SOON AS POSSIBLE. My boss has got it out for her."

"But they can't question her without a guardian present, right?"

"Right, but my boss ain't playing by the rules. Where the fuck is Lil Mama? Find her."

"I'm gonna hit her phone and then hit you back."

"Hurry up, E!"

Young Meech

I feel as if I'm in pure hell. Every woman that I have ever loved is gone. My boo, Tyesha, died at the hands of my best friend. How could I have been that stupid? I should have killed his ass at the bank. Lil Man killed my Auntie Shawn and my sister, Tiki, in the same night. How can I ever recover from that? That same night, I also killed my mother. I don't regret that. That bitch deserved to die. She had my father killed, and she was fucking his best friend. My heart was so cold. I'm going to kill everybody that shares the same bloodline as that nigga—kids and all. If I can't get HIM, I'm getting everybody he loves. *ring ring*

"Yo?"

"Young, this ReRe? You a'ight?"

"Hell naw! Fuck you mean? That nigga took everything from me."

"You still got me and E, baby."

"I know and I appreciate that. Where JuJu at? She didn't come to the burial."

"You don't know?"

"What now, man?"

"The police picked her up and charged her with Tiki and Tae's murder."

"Never!"

"Yes they did. We're trying to find Lil Mama right now. Have you seen her?"

"N-n-naw. Hit her phone."

12

"Where you at? Come slide on me, Meech. Meet me at me and Poohman's crib."

Boo

This person lying before me was not my lil sister. It couldn't be. She was in a full body cast. Her face was raw with blisters everywhere, and she was on a ventilator machine.

"Oh God, Lil Mama, pull through this."

The nurse told me that her body was so badly burned that they had to put her in a medically induced coma. The crash itself broke four ribs, and they had to remove her spleen.

"I know you can hear me. I heard you when I was in my coma. Push through this shit, lil girl. I need you. Ju's in trouble. She needs you. You are going to be fine, baby. I love you. Fight sis." The machines began beeping excitedly.

"Nurse, get in here now!"

The nurses and doctors came running in to assist her. All I could think about was Lil Mama's ass fighting to come out of that coma. They kicked me out of the room so they could work on her. I decided to call Jaw. I needed all the support right now.

"Hey Auntie, what's good?"

"Come up to Holy Christ."

"Who up there?"

"Lil Mama."

"Say no more. I'm on the way."

"Bring yo momma."

Thirty minutes later, Heidi, Jaw, Poohman, and I sat in the waiting room waiting for the doctor to come tell us that she was all right. Heidi was the first one to speak.

"I'm gonna kick her skinny ass for having us worry like this."

"I know right? I been here all day."

Jaw hugged me.

"Auntie, what the hell happened?"

"I called her after they took JuJu at the funeral."

Heidi appeared confused.

"Who took JuJu?"

"Let me finish. The police told me that she was under arrest for the murders of Tiki and Tae. I called Lil Mama to let her know what was going on. While we were on the phone, she said that she was about to come back. She said she was about to bust a U-turn, but her brakes didn't work."

Heidi was pacing now.

"Well, Boo, what happened?"

"Stop interrupting me hoe, damn. After she said she couldn't stop, I heard her scream my name and the line went dead."

Just then, the doctor came out looking as if he had run a marathon. I was the first one to close the distance between us.

"Bout time, doc. Is she all right? I need to see her."

He grabbed my hand and held it too tight for my liking.

"This never gets easy. I did my very best to save her, but I couldn't. I'm sorry, she's gone."

It took me a minute to process what the fuck he had said. I turned to look at Heidi, Jaw, and Poohman and they were each crying. The shit still didn't hit me. I walked to Jaw and wiped his tears.

"Stop crying, it's okay."

He held me tenderly.

"Auntie, he just said that she was gone!"

My head began spinning. My legs became weak, and I dropped to my knees. It was as if a light bulb clicked in my head. I screamed, "LIL MAMA, WHY BABY WHY?" I broke down.

"Jaw please tell me he lying. Not my lil sister. I need to see her."

I jumped up and ran to the room they had her in. She was surely lying there, dead!

JoJo

Maybe I bit off more that I could chew dealing with Lil Man. That nigga is truly disturbed. I was down with getting my hands dirty, but the nigga is seriously trying to wipe out the whole Eastside of Chicago. I was going to avenge the deaths of my brothers and my cousin, Big Moe. I just needed to find a way to get rid of him. He was not to be trusted. To add fuel to the fire, I messed around and gave him some coochie. Why the hell did I do that? Now he really won't be trying to go anywhere. Ole stankin' ass lil boy. I broke down and told my sister everything that was going on. She was definitely onboard with getting revenge for our family. We had a plan to get them E.S.C bitches. We just didn't need Lil Man to do it. JuJu was already in jail. We came up with the perfect plan to get JuJu back. I had something special for Dirty's ass. That hoe drugged me and was about to kill me, had she not received that phone call. Her mistake was allowing me to live. I was going to get her ass if it was the last thing I did. So for

16

now, Mia and me I were trying to get Jaw to handle Lil Man. I told Mia to call Jaw and tell him that Lil Man was the reason that JuJu was sitting in jail. I know he was going to kill Lil Man eventually. We just wanted to speed up the process. After he killed Lil Man, he was going to die too. But until our plan was in motion, I had to play nice with his lil creepy ass. Ugh! Speaking of the devil...

"JoJo, what's up? I'm hungry."

"You need to take a shower. You smell like a skunk sprayed yo ass."

He began giggling like a kid.

"Damn bitch, that was rude. I should make you suck my dick while I'm smelling like a skunk, you disrespectful ass bitch."

Now I had to do damage control. For he to be a cold-blooded murderer, he sho' was sensitive.

"I was just playing, Boo. Damn! Chill out! Go get in the shower while I make you something to eat, okay?"

"Quit playing so much. Make me some chicken fingers and French fries."

"Yeah, you can come upstairs and wash me up like my mommy used to."

I just rolled my eyes. His mother was a sick ass bitch. The bitch was still washing him up until the day she died, which was like two months ago.

The nigga, a teenager! I mean like what the fuck!"

17

FOUR

Detective Malone

"Sir, we got the double murder suspect in the interrogating room."

"Okay, did you ask her if she was hungry?"

"Umm, she told me to go fuck myself, and then she lawyered up."

"We got us a feisty one, huh? Fuck it. Turn the air up and let that little bitch freeze. I'm going to take a nap."

I closed my office door and lay down on the couch. I was trying to relax, so I closed my eyes thinking I was about to get me a good ole nap. I was about to dose off when I heard a loud commotion outside my office door.

"What the hell?" I swung open my door trying to see what the hell was going on.

"Bishop? What the fuck is all the noise?"

He was laughing so hard that he was on the verge of tears.

"Well? Spit it out, damn it."

"That lil girl just kicked Sanchez in the balls."

"What? Why?"

"Because he went in there fucking with her. He tried to play the bad cop by telling her if she didn't act right, she was going to go to jail for the rest of her life. You know ... the usual. Well, when he slapped his hands down on the desk, that little bitch snapped."

I shook my head.

"So what you're trying to tell me is that I can't even take a nap because y'all stupid motha fuckas can't control a child?"

Still laughing, he smiled.

"Boss, that lil bitch kicks better than David Beckham."

"Get the fuck outta my damn face. I bet your kids run you at home, pussy!"

I was beyond pissed. I stormed into the interrogating room.

"Listen to me, you little murderer. If you put your hands or feet on another one of my officers, I'm going to personally beat your ass. Do I make myself clear?"

The nerve of these disrespectful kids these days. That little bitch cocked her head to the side and spit at me.

"Did you just spit at me, little girl?"

"Fuck you! I want my lawyer. I'm not answering shit, you fat bastard. I'm going to sue them short ass pants off of you. I WANT MY LAWYER!"

Call me crazy, but I was actually shocked that she spoke to me like that.

"Oh, I got something for you, you little ignorant bitch."

"Damn, Boo, answer the phone ... shit."

I was just about to hang up when I heard a dude's voice.

"Hello? Where's Boo? Who's is this?"

"Chill E. It's me, Jaw."

"Jaw, they got Ju up at the police station. Ash told me to hurry up and find her a lawyer fast. Where the fuck is Lil Mama? They up there tryin' to do her dirty. She need an adult up there with her."

I'm doing all this talking and he was just quiet. Too quiet.

"Nigga, I know you."

"Lil Mama is dead." Did I hear him right?

"What you just say?"

"You heard me, Dirty. She didn't make it."

"Make it from what? What the fuck happen?"

"Somebody cut her brakes, and she crashed into a big ass semi-truck. Her body was burned real badly. The doctors tried to save her but they couldn't."

I sat there for like a moment straight and then began to cry my eyes out. That lady was like my mother. We don't need this shit right now. I couldn't hold back the sobs that escaped the back of my throat.

"Wh ... who gon' tell Ju?"

I broke down. It took me a few minutes to get myself under control. It didn't help that I heard Jaw crying on the other end of the phone.

"Jaw, somebody needs to be up there with her."

"I'm gonna send my mom dukes. As for the lawyer, call this number..."

I hung up the phone and called to break the bad news to Re.

"Hey bestie, what's good?"

"Re, Lil Mama just died."

The phone went silent for what seemed like forever.

"Hello?"

"I'm here. I don't know what to say. Where is Ju?"

"At the police station on 103rd. Call this number. She needs a lawyer AS SOON AS POSSIBLE. Jaw sent his mother up there to be with her. Give the lawyer whatever he want."

"A'ight. Re, you good?"

"I'm good. I'm just numb right now. I don't have time to be sad."

"Why is that? It's ok to show some emotion."

"I can't be in a sad mood because I got a lot of killing to do."

"Not over this phone you don't." *click*

Damn, my bestie gon' flip when she find out about her auntie. I was on the verge of crying once more. I had to pull myself together. I needed to drop by my crib and grab some serious dough to pay this lawyer. We needed the best lawyer in town because we were in for the fight of our lives.

Heidi

I need a damn drink. All this shit is just too much. First Tiki and Shawn ... now Lil Mama. It might have seemed like we didn't get along, but on the low I liked her a lot. That lil skinny bitch was a true gangsta for real. Plus, Boo fucked with her the long way. I had to be strong for my sister. She was crazy about Lil Mama. To see her cry like that broke me down in a major way. It's been about two hours since the doctor broke the news about her. Boo has been in the same spot by her bedside, just looking at that shit tears me up. Now wait a damn minute. I'm not scared of the dead, but I am not--and I mean *not* about to be all up in there hugging and kissing on them like she in there doing. Enough is enough! I walked in the room and put my hand on her shoulder.

"Come on sis, it's time to go. They need to clear the room out."

Poor baby was a mess.

"I-I-I can't just leave her like that, Heidi. She didn't leave me. I gotta stay with her."

This was going to be harder than I thought.

"I know Boo, but you wasn't dead. She is, baby. Now don't make me drag yo ass outta here."

I wrapped my arms around her and surprisingly she walked with me.

"Jaw, take her home. I'm going to the liquor store."

"Naw ma, I need you to go up there to the police station and see about JuJu for me."

"The police station? What the fuck?"

"She needs a guardian up there with her."

"That poor baby. Okay, you go to the liquor store and get me and Boo some Old English and a pint of Remy."

"I'll meet you at the station, ma."

Fifteen minutes later, I walked into the third district police precinct. This shit was so outta character for me. I'm from the projects. We don't just voluntarily walk into the police station. When I walked up to the reception desk, there was a fat, black ass bitch with a bogus lace front, lime green Freddy Krueger nails, and fire engine red lipstick. She had the nerve to look at me and roll her eyes. And if that wasn't enough, she gave me the one-minute gesture and went back to talking on the phone. I was appalled. Unprofessional ass bitch.

"So you telling me that I can get a tummy tuck, lipo, and a breast reduction all for $3,000? Bitch, where? I can do that. You know I been saving up ever since I put that nigga Pistol P out. Girl, yes I was tired of his shit."

I had had enough of listening to that bullshit.

"Excuse me? While you on the motherfucking phone bumping yo big ass gums, I want you to tell me why the fuck my child has been up here for over five hours and ain't nobody called me?"

She smacked her lips and turned her chair around.

"Miracle ... girl, let me call you back. All right bye."

I guess she needed a moment to get that hood-rat shit outta her system. When she turned back around, she came correct.

"I'm sorry, what's your daughter's name?"

"Ja'ziya Campbell. She was brought in almost five hours ago."

She typed something on her keyboard. Something must have popped up because her eyes grew large.

"Um, do you know that she's charged with two murders?"

"What I do know is that y'all had my baby in custody without contacting her guardian. I smell a motha-fucking lawsuit. Take me to my damn baby. NOW!"

She jumped her fat ass up and told me to follow her. I couldn't help but laugh at her. She was so fat that her knees rubbed against each other, causing her pants to flood. She walked me into a room that was so cold that I could see my own breath in front of me. When I saw JuJu balled up in the corner with her arms inside of her shirt, I snapped: "Aw, y'all think this is an episode of the First 48?"

"Ma'am, what are you talking about?"

"Why the fuck is this room so cold? You trying to freeze a confession outta her? Turn this damn air off and get your supervisor."

I walked up to JuJu and gave her my jacket.

"Thank you He-."

"Call me mama and whisper. You know they are listening through that thick ass mirror glass."

"I been asking for a lawyer since the ride over here. They still came in here trying to talk to me. I kicked some asshole in his nuts. I think his name was Sanchez."

I started laughing.

"Why'd you kick him?"

"Because he came in here talking cash money shit to me."

"Oh yeah?"

"Yeah."

Suddenly the door flew open. In walked a fat, old, bald-headed nigga with a cigar in his mouth. He looked me up and down before I spoke.

"Hello. How are you? I'm Detective Malone."

"So you'll be the one I name in our lawsuit?"

"Lawsuit?"

"Hell yeah. My baby lawyered up hours ago. You put her in this cold ass room and turned the air up higher. That's cruel and inhumane, bastard. Not to mention you didn't call her guardian."

"No need for name calling. Let's just settle down here."

"Settle down my ass. You violated her rights, and you're going to pay for that. Now is she under arrest or wanted for questioning?"

"She's under arrest. We have some very strong evidence on her."

"Like what?"

"All I can day is that her fingerprints are all over the crime scene."

Before I could say another word, JuJu snapped, "Since you so gah damn smart, you would have also known that the reason why my fingerprints are all over the house is because I LIVE THERE!"

He was stuck for a second. Not knowing what else to say, he turned to leave. Before he closed the door, he said, "I got an eyewitness that puts you there at the time of the murder."

When he left, I pulled her close. I thought about telling her about Lil Mama but decided to wait to see if she would get a bond. Where the hell was E with that damn lawyer?

FIVE

Chapter

Mia

"JoJo? I'm about to hit the mall. You wanna go?"

"No because Lil Man gon' wanna come. Just buy me something to wear for Christmas."

"All right."

I'll never understand why she won't just leave his ass in a ditch somewhere. I mean, really, his scrawny ass ain't that tough. Oh by the way, I'm Mia—the one and only. I'm 21 years old, and I've been on my own for a very long time. My mother was murderer by her boyfriend when I was younger. I was raised with my brothers, J.R. and Boogie. They taught me how to survive on these streets. I was getting so much money I had to move outta the Cabrini Green projects. Those niggas over there started noticing my come up. So it was time to move around. I moved over east and set up shop. I've been doing the damn thang without any problems. It's been a hard few years. My G-ma died, and then Boogie and J.R. were killed. When I lost my brothers, I was ready to give up on the dope game. I loved my brothers. When I needed them, they were always there. I knew it was a matter of time before somebody killed Ramone's shyster ass. I tried to tell my brothers about him and his ways a long time ago. Don't get me wrong, I loved my cousin, but Lord knows he wasn't right. Just because he was a fucked-up person, it doesn't mean that I was going to let his death go unavenged. If that was a thought, then y'all got me fucked up. I ain't scared to body a nigga. They don't call me Murda Mia for nothing. I caught my first body a few years ago. I loved him. Maybe I loved him too much. Maybe for him, my love wasn't enough. I'll never know. It was five years ago, and I was on my way to his stash house to drop off that day's take. I was missing my baby; I hadn't spoken to him all day. I didn't trip on him because he stayed busy, but lately he had been different. I had been with that man since we were like six and seven. I'm talking about some grade-school type of love, so I knew him better than he knew himself. I hit him on his phone just to say hi.

"Yo?"

"Yo nothing. What's good, baby? I miss you. Where you at?"

"Where you at?"

"On my way to the drop spot."

"For what?"

"Why else would I go to the spot, Tre?"

That question sent my antennas to the roof. He always thought he was slick, but not tonight. I was going to crack this cold case file.

"Tre, you tripping. You want me to just go home so you come get the money and make the drop yourself?"

"Yeah, go home. Meet you there."

"A'ight, I love you."

"I know." *click*

Yeah that nigga had me fucked up. First off, he always told me to never bring money to where we laid our head. Yeah, something was definitely going on with that nigga. When I pulled up to the stash house, there were two cars in the driveway. His car and one I never saw before.

"This nigga got me fucked all the way up!"

Now Boogie told me to never let a nigga play with my feelings. So if Tre was doing something that he knew he had no business doing, I was popping his ass. I walked up to the side of the house and peeked through the dining room window looking for something out of order. I stood there for several minutes feeling stupid. I felt dumb for not trusting my boo. I walked to the front door and was about to stick the key in when the door came flying open.

"Aw shit, girl, you scared the hell out of me."

I stood there frozen. The bitch was half-naked with just a tee shirt on.

"Where Tre at?"

"Who are you? One of his workers?"

What? One of his workers? I'm about to kill both of these motha fuckers.

"Yeah, I gotta drop some bread off to him."

"Aw, okay, girl. He in there ... in the bedroom. You can go in there. I'm about to get some weed outta the car if you wanna blow something."

"Who are you again?"

"My bad, I'm his girlfriend, Shaya."

I walked in the crib and headed straight for the bedroom.

"Shay? Hurry up so I can finish wearing that ass out."

"Oh yeah, Tre?"

The nigga's eyes grew so big that you would have thought that he had just won the lottery.

"M-M-Mia! What's good, ma? Why you not at the crib?"

"Really? After all this time, this how you do me."

I reached in my bag and grabbed my gun that he bought me in case of emergencies. I looked him dead in his eyes, and for the first time I saw something I never thought I'd ever see ... fear! I was really trying to keep my composure.

"You a foul ass nigga."

I heard footsteps behind me so I turned around to see his bitch Shaya standing there. When she saw the gun, she began pleading her case.

"Please don't hurt us. My boyfriend has money. You can have whatever you want. Tell her, Tre."

He dropped his head because he knew that he had just fucked up.

"Shut the fuck up. Mia baby, please!"

"Baby? Why the fuck are you calling..." I had heard enough. *pop pop.* I shot that bitch in her chest twice. Tre jumped up asshole naked. The thought of me knowing that he was just fucking this bitch enraged me.

"Mia, please don't. I love you."

"I'm getting an abortion."

"You pregnant?" *pop pop pop.*

I shot and killed the love of my life that night. I don't even know if the bitch survived. I took all the dope and money he had, which totaled over a million combined and dipped. Back to the present. I wondered what was going through JoJo's head. She was not built for this murder shit. I'm going to have to keep my eyes on her. Driving to the mall, I had a lot of things on my mind. If what JoJo said was true, then the Eastside Crazy bitches were responsible for killing J.R., Boogie, and Ramone: I was going to personally fuck their worlds up. With JuJu being locked up and Tiki dead, it wasn't going to be that hard. I mean, really, how hard was it going to be to kill some damn kids?

28

Damn, the mall was packed. I hated shopping around the holidays. I scanned the lot for a parking spot. *Bingo.* It was a Red Honda Civic pulling out. While I was patiently waiting for the car to pull out, a Baby Blue Charger with some 22-inch rims came outta nowhere and zoomed into my spot.

"Oh no the fuck that nigga didn't!

I pulled directly in front of him, blocking him in as I jumped out. I walked to the driver-side door and was about to bang on the window when the door opened. Out came this ole sexy chocolate thang. I had to catch my breath. He was tall, like 6 feet 2 or something like that. His dreads were neat and fresh. He had these dark mysterious eyes that made me melt instantly. Focus bitch. This nigga just stole your parking spot.

"Excuse me; I know damn well you saw me about to park there?"

"I didn't see you. You want me to move, shawty?"

He was so sexy I was stuck.

"Hello? I said do you want me to move?"

"I mean that would be the right thing to do." While we were going back and forth, the car next to him was getting ready to back out.

"Hold on, ma, this car 'bout to move. How 'bout I hold the spot for you. Go get in your car and come on."

I couldn't do shit but smile.

"I mean it's the least you can do, parking spot thief."

He laughed and watched me walk back to my car. You know since I knew he was looking, I had to throw that ass in a circle, right? I mean at 5'5 and 155 pounds, I'm slugging over here. I pulled into the spot next to him and got out.

"Thank you for holding it for me. I'm sorry; I didn't get your name. I'm Mia."

"My bad. My name is L.J. It was nice meeting you, Mia. You have a nice day."

"Damn, I can't get a number on you?"

He smiled so hard I saw the sexiest dimple in his left cheek.

"Yeah ma, it ain't nothing. Give me your number and I'm gonna call you right now."

After we exchanged numbers, we then said our goodbyes. I hope he calls me. He was fine as shit. Maybe I can jump on some dick for Christmas. Ho Ho Ho!

SIX

Chapter

Lock Jaw

Today the lawyer visited JuJu. He told her the case was weak, but the judge didn't think so. He denied bond. The lawyer said that he was going to push for a speedy trial. That should get my boo in court in like three months. I didn't want to bring the New Year in by myself, but it was looking as if I had no choice. I went ahead and put three stacks on her books to hold her over until the trial. She should be a'ight. I hate that shit for her though. And if things couldn't get any worse, she was being charged as an adult. My boo was facing life in prison without parole. The lawyer told me that the state had a solid witness by the name of Derrick Walker. I'm sure that he and Lil Man are the same person. Without Lil Man, they had no case. I had to find that nigga. *ring ring*

"Who is this private number calling me?"

"You have a collect call from Ja'ziya Campbell. Press five to accept the call."

"Hello, what's good, baby? You good, love?"

"I'm okay. The lawyer said the case was weak without..."

"We ain't gotta talk about that shit right now. When is your visiting day?"

"Tomorrow."

"I'm going to come up there and see you, boo."

"Bay, have you heard from my Auntie, Lil Mama? I've been blowing her phone up, but she's not picking up and that is so not like her. Is everything ok?"

Damn! That shit just hurt my heart. How in the world am I supposed to tell her that her auntie is gone? I don't want to lie to her, but for now, I'm going to have to.

"She went outta town to handle something for Boo. She must not have no service because she ain't picking up for us neither."

"Does she know what's going on?"

"Of course she knows. How you doing in there? Them hoes ain't in there fucking with you are they?"

"Naw, I'm good. It's a few BD chicks in here from South Shore that I'm cool with, so I'm good."

"Damn, I miss you, ma. I can't wait 'til you come home."

"You have 1 minute remaining."

"I'm going to call you in the morning Jaw. Come about 8:30."

"All right, Boo. I love you, and keep your head to the sky."

That was so hard on me man. I wish I could go up there and get my girl. I needed to get outta the house, so I hopped in the shower and freshened myself to death. I was about to hit the mall and do a little Christmas shopping. After making sure I was the shit in the mirror, I grabbed my keys and hit the streets. I turned on the radio, and then began juking like shit.

They was playing that *Pullin' Up* by Meek Mill and the Weekend: "Tell ya man wait inside when I'm pullin' up." That shit go so hard. I made it to the mall in no time.

Damn, all these fucking people. I hated shopping. I saw a Honda Civics' reverse lights turn on so I readied to zoom in there.

I peeped this Black Lexus waiting. Man, shawty was about to be outta luck. As soon as the Civic pulled out, I let that Hemi roar. I zoomed right into the parking spot. I tried to hide the smile on my face, when ole girl parked behind me and made her way to my driver's side door. When I stepped outta the car, she looked mad. She was staring hard as shit. I guess she was admiring a nigga because I had my shit together. I never stepped outta the crib bogus. I guess she finally found her voice.

"Excuse me. I know damn well you saw me about to park there."

"I didn't see you, you want me to move, shawty?"

The bitch made me feel famous because she kept on staring at me.

"Hello? I said do you want me to move?"

"I mean that would be the right thing to do."

That hoe was outta her rabbit ass mind, because I was not moving. I was about to say something when the alarm on the Cadillac beeped next to us.

"Hold on, ma! How 'bout I hold the spot for you. Go get in your car and come on."

"I mean it's the least you can do, parking spot thief."

I had to laugh at the last comment. I'm naturally an ass man, so when she walked off to go get her car, I had to see what she was working with. She knew I was watching because she was throwing that ass like a quarterback. Down boy. I was a taken man. She pulled in and got back out.

"Thank you for holding it for me. I'm sorry I didn't get your name. I'm Mia."

"My bad. My name is L.J. You have a nice day."

"Damn, I can't get a number on you?" I laughed at her boldness.

33

"Yeah ma, it ain't nothin'. Give me your number and I'ma call you right now."

After we said our goodbyes, I did my shopping in less than two hours. I grabbed a slice of Sbarro's pizza and headed back to my car. I was just about to pull off when my phone rang.

"Yo?"

"Jaw?"

"Who dis?"

"Re, why are you answering Poohman's phone?"

"Damn I must have grabbed his by mistake. He at my crib though."

"Um, uh, I bet."

"Call my phone, girl. I bet he answers. A, yo ass crazy."

"You better know it! Bye."

Aw shit. I hope ole girl don't call that phone. I hit the expressway and made my way to my mother's crib. When I pulled up, I saw a group of niggas outside her building. I reached under my seat and grabbed my pistol, just in case. When I got outta the car, I noticed that two of them niggas was my little brothers, Outlaw and Money Man.

"Money Man? What y'all doing? Come help me get these bags outta the trunk."

Money Man waved me over.

"Hold on bro. We battling. I'm 'bout to eat this nigga alive. He said he can rap better than me."

I walked over to them because I wanted to hear him spit. I looked at him and nodded my head.

"A'ight then, eat his ass up."

When I tell you that my lil brother devoured that boy. Dude was so salty that he looked like he wanted to cry. I had to intervene before things got out of hand.

"A'ight, come on and help me with y'all gifts."

When I walked back to the car to grab some bags I turned to see if my lil brothers were behind me. That's when I saw the dude that Money Man beat in the rap battle go in his coat and pull out a big ass gun.

"MONEY MAN!"

boc boc

It was too late. He hit Money Man in the side. I ran to grab my lil brother off the ground when I saw Outlaw creep up behind the nigga that had just shot Money Man.

"Outlaw, NOOOO!"

He shot the dude in the back and it made a red shower of blood, because everything flew outta his chest. I scooped Money Man up and rushed him to the hospital. So much for getting into the Christmas spirit.

I have lost a lot of people in my life, but planning this girl's funeral by far was the hardest thing I ever had to do. Heidi has been my rock. She's the one that has been getting everything together. The only thing left to do was pick out the casket.

"Heidi, can you please do it. I don't want to."

"Don't worry I got you. When are you going to tell JuJu?"

"I can't right now. That girl gon' go crazy up in that place. I just can't do her like that."

"A'ight, but she needs to know soon." *ring ring*

"Boo, hand me my phone please."

"Hello. WHAT? I'm on the way."

I looked at Heidi and knew it was bad news. Shit I was scared to ask.

"Let's go. Money Man just got shot!"

"Please tell me there's not about to be another funeral."

"Oh, it is, but we not burying Heidi's finest!"

The ride to the hospital was quiet. Too quiet if you asked me. I knew this lady well. She hadn't told me everything.

"Money Man, a'ight?"

"Girl, he fine. I'm just worried about Outlaw."

"Outlaw? What happened to him?"

She just gave me a sideway glance that told me that she had, in fact, not told me everything.

"Spit that shit out."

"Well, right after Money Man went down, Outlaw came up behind the nigga and shot him."

I just put my head down.

"We don't need this shit right now. I mean we still gotta bury Lil Mama, and I pray to God that the lawyer can get JuJu home. Now we have to worry about if somebody saw Lil Rambo shoot that boy."

Heidi paused for a few seconds.

"Bitch, who the hell is Rambo?" I rolled my eyes at her slow ass.

"Man shut up."

When we finally got to the hospital, Jaw was waiting for us at the ER entrance.

"What's up, auntie? He cool. It went straight through his side without touching any organs."

"What the hell happened?"

"When I pulled up, he was in a heated ass rap battle. I let him do his thang. He embarrassed the shit outta the dude, and I guess the guy got mad. He ain't waste no time pulling out and shooting

36

him."

Heidi jumped in.

"Where the hell is Outlaw?"

"I got his lil trigger-happy ass stashed away at my crib. Poohman is keeping him company."

With all of this drama going on, I still haven't mustered up the courage to tell JuJu that her damn auntie was dead.

SEVEN

Chapter

Lil Man

I've been laying low for a few weeks now. That police dude told me that Ju's trial date was set for March 9. That was less than three months away. I know you might think I'm a sucker for testifying on JuJu at her trial, but y'all gotta understand that the Eastside Crazy hoes declared war when they killed my brother. So now, it was my turn to finish what they started. *ring ring*

"Hello?"

"You know you a dead ass nigga when I see you, right?"

"Young? What's good boy? How has life been treating you?"

"You's a funny ass nigga, but I bet you I'ma have the last laugh."

"We'll see about that buddy. See you in the streets." *Click*

At this point, there was no need to lip box over the phone. It is what it is. I knew eventually I was gonna have to see that nigga. He better be ready. Sitting in the house was torture when I was so used to terrorizing the streets. I decided to hit up Facebook. Maybe I could find some action. It amazes me how these dumb ass people put their business on here. I thought about looking up Dirty to see if she was as dumb as the rest of these people. After about 10 minutes of searching, I got lucky.

"Jackpot."

She wrote, '*What's good, Chicago? Me and my ride-or-die ReRe 'bout to head up to the county to see our bestie. Free JuJu.*'

Damn I could kill two birds with one stone.

"Ay, JoJo?"

"Huh? Why you wake me up? I'm tired."

"Tired from what? You don't do shit. Lazy ass! Come on, I know where Dirty and that other bitch 'bout to be."

"Ok, go get 'em then." I punched her ass in her back as hard as hell.

"OUCH! Don't fucking hit me like that no more bastard."

"Then get yo ass up. We in this shit together."

After a few lip smacks and eye rolls, she finally jumped in the shower. I might as well get some pussy before we go. I busted into the bathroom like a thief in the night. I could tell I scared her because she dropped the soap.

"Stay in that position!"

I quickly got my rocks off. I felt different afterwards. I felt like her body had finally received me.

"Get dressed and be ready in 10 minutes."

Dirty E

"Come on Re. We gotta be there before the shift change."

Women take forever getting ready. Poohman was about to take us up to the county to see JuJu. I decided that I was going to tell her about her auntie. Fuck that. She needed to know. Especially since we knew for sure that she wasn't getting out. After about 30 more minutes, we were finally on our way. Re and Poohman seemed distant.

39

"Re, you a'ight?"

"Hell naw! I'm mad as hell because that lawyer wanted 10-G's just to retain his ass. To represent her, he wants almost $100,000, E. He couldn't even get her out on bond."

"He better get her off with that kind of bread in the air."

"I know, right? When are we gonna start looking for that nigga Lil Man and that bitch JoJo?"

"After we go up here and holla at JuJu, we can go on the prowl if you want."

We made it to the county right on time. It was early, and there wasn't too much traffic. Finding a parking spot was damn near impossible though.

"Poohman, right there. Hurry up."

He zoomed right into a parking spot in front of the building. Damn we got lucky.

"Come on y'all, its 7:25. We need to hurry up and make it through the gate."

Lil Man

I was asking for trouble. Not only was I up here at the county jail to commit a few murders, but I was also in a stolen car. I loved living on the edge. After I kill those bitches, I think I'll take a trip to go see Young.

"JoJo, ain't that them over there crossing the street?"

She sat up and squinted her eyes.

"Yep, that's them. What you 'bout to do?"

"What you mean? I'ma wait on them to come out. When they do, it's on!"

ReRe

I could never get used to this shit. I had to walk through this big ass machine. I was curious, so I asked the police lady what the machine did.

"It scans your body for contraband and drugs."

I was so glad I didn't smoke weed this morning. After going through a series of doors and hallways, we were finally led into a room containing windows with phones on the wall. I assumed it was the visiting room. So much for being able to hug my girl.

"This is how we gotta talk to her, Poohman?"

He hugged me.

"Yeah ma, no contact visits in here."

E was in her own world. We haven't ever finished mourning the loss of Tiki, and here we are in a jail visiting our other bestie. This shit was all bad. I heard a door open and in walked Ju.

"Damn she look bogus."

I couldn't believe that I said that shit out loud, but it was true. Her hair was dry and brittle looking. She looked like she had even loss a few pounds. I was the first one to walk up to the glass and pick the phone up.

"Hey Ju, you look like shit."

"Thanks girl I try. I'm good, just ready to get the fuck up outta here. My trial date is in March. That's like 82 days away. This place is nasty. Bitch, they got green bologna."

"Green bologna? Aw hell naw. Don't eat it."

"I'm not. Why you think I look so small? I miss my boo. Why he ain't come with yell?'

"I think something happened to his brother. He's at the hospital."

41

"Where is my auntie? I need her."

"Hold on, E wanna talk to you."

I turned towards E and gave her that look that she knew oh so well. I was not about to be the bearer of bad news. She was the man, well the woman, for that job.

"Ju baby, what's crackin'? You look good."

"You're a liar and a fat mouth. I know I look like shit. Where is my auntie?"

I saw E put her head down, so I knew that shit was about to hit the fan. I just hugged Poohman and held my breath.

"Ju, um I love you, baby, and we're going to get through this."

"Get through what?"

"Lil Mama got into a car accident after Tiki's funeral. Sh ... she didn't make..." *Boom*

E never finished the statement. JuJu snapped! She hit the glass so hard I thought she broke her hand.

"NO, DON'T SAY THAT! PLEASE GOD NO!"

That shit broke my heart. Officers came from everywhere trying to restrain her. She gave their ass the blues. It was hard to watch.

"Excuse me?" I turned around to see two officers standing behind me.

"What?"

"What the hell did y'all say to her?"

"Family business."

"Well your family business has disrupted my visiting room. Y'all gotta go!"

I hated to have to leave her in there like that, but at least she knew. Hopefully we can get her out for the funeral. E took that scene to heart.

"E, baby, you good?"

"I'm trying not to cry. That shit fucked me up."

Leaving the building, I felt as if a storm was brewing in the city. I was ready for whatever.

Lil Man

Damn, they've been in there for almost two hours. I wish they'd hurry up so they can die. Shit! As soon as I see them come out, I'm going to pull a good ole-fashioned drive-by.

"JoJo you better get ready to run in case I crash this motha fucka."

The way she looked at me pissed me off.

"What the fuck was that look about?"

"I want them too, but in broad daylight? And in front of this big ass jail? That's stupid."

She was right, but when the opportunity presents itself you take it damn it.

"They're dying today. End of discussion."

"We gon' end up in jail like that bitch."

No sooner than she said it, that I saw them coming out of the gate.

"JoJo, you ready?"

"Let's go."

I put the pedal to the metal flying down the street.

"Grab the wheel."

Dirty E

I couldn't wait to get back to the hood. I hope that Ju beat that case man. Man, I ... I looked to my left and saw this car flying down the street driving right towards us.

"Re, what the ... OH SHIT, RUN!"

Lil Man had his head and half his body hanging out of the window with a big ass gun in his hand. "DIE BITCHES!" *BOC-BOC-BOC-BOC*

Oh my goodness. That nigga ill. I took off running across the street, and Poohman and Re ran towards the car on 27th Street. We were unarmed and in trouble. When I turned around, he was on my ass. The nigga jumped the curb and was now driving on the sidewalk. Where the hell was the police when you needed them? I ran in Popeye's Chicken, which was across the street from the courthouse. I thought that he was going to run into the building, but he didn't. He turned off and disappeared. This shit had gone on long enough. It was time for that nigga to die. Poohman and Re pulled up on me as soon as I walked outta Popeye's. I looked around before I jumped in the car.

"Y'all see that shit? That nigga gotta go. I mean that shit." I was on fire.

"Re, how the fuck he even know we was up here?"

"Your guess is as good as mine. Let's go. I need to call and check on Young."

EIGHT

Chapter

Young Meech

After all the shit that Lil Man did, you would have thought that he would have done a better job at keeping his family safe. I had been watching his sister, Bessie, for the last week. She leaves for school at 7:30 every morning. After school, she and two friends walk to her auntie's job. From there, Bessie and the auntie walk to 87th and Exchange to the babysitter to pick up the auntie's two little boys, Julius and Demand. From there they go back home. Today was the same routine. The only difference about today was it was going to be the last day that they did anything. *ring ring*

I wasn't going to answer it until I saw it was Re.

"Yo, what's good girl?"

"I was just calling to check on you."

"I'm good why?"

"Lil Man just tried to shoot Dirty, Poohman, and me in front of the county jail on 26th and California."

"Oh yeah?"

"Hell yeah. He's doing too much. I want his ass."

"I'm 'bout to hit him where it hurts the most. Let me hit you back."

"Be careful."

"Yup."

I rode up on Julie and Bessie to see if they wanted a ride.

"Bessie, y'all want a ride home?"

"Yeah, thank you."

Lil Man must not have been talking to them about our beefs, because they were happy to see me. Bessie sat in the front. I knew that she had a little crush on me.

"Hey Young, I'm sorry about Tiki. Where you been?"

"I been around. Where yo brother at? He ain't answering his phone."

"I have no idea. He's been staying with his little girlfriend over there on 84th and Burnham. He comes around every other day,"

That was all I needed to know. Ten minutes later, I was walking outta her auntie's crib. I wondered how long it was going to take before the whole house went up in flames. I went straight to the crib to change. I got gasoline all over my damn shoes. I waited about 30 minutes and turned to Channel 7 News. When I saw breaking news, I decided to place a call.

"Who the fuck is this calling me private, like a little bitch?" I laughed.

"Turn to channel 7, pussy ass nigga." *click*

Lil Man

"JoJo, Turn the T.V. to channel 7, quick!"

"Why? I'm watching *Law and Order*." *Whack!*

I slapped the shit outta her ass. Her mouth was getting on my nerves. *Whack!*

46

"What the fuck?"

That bitch hit me back and took off running.

"I'm beating yo ass, bitch."

"Catch me first."

I had to laugh at her ass. I turned to channel 7 and watched the news that was on.

"Just in, I'm Cheryl Love reporting from Channel 7 News. Sad day for a family of four found dead in their Eastside home behind me. Just after 3:00 p.m., neighbors reported that they smelled smoke. When police arrived, the building was engulfed in flames. After the fire was put out, the bodies of four people were found. Two of the bodies are believed to be small children. According to the police, the fire was deliberately set. That's all the police are saying right now. Please, if you have any information on this heinous crime, I urge you to call Crime Stoppers. You can remain anonymous."

I clicked off the T.V. and sat there for a few minutes numb. It can't be. Please let it be somebody else. I picked up my phone and called my auntie. No answer.

I called this dude named Skee that lived next door to my auntie.

"Hello?"

"Aye, Skee, this Lil Man."

"Man, Joe, where the fuck you at? They just found Julie, Bessie, Julius, and Demond dead."

I couldn't hold back my rage "NOOOO! FUCK! I'MA KILL THAT NIGGA."

I decided to call Re and Dirty and put them up on game.

"Hello, Re?"

"Yeah, what's up lil boy?"

"Watch y'all backs. I may have just started World War 3."

"What you mean?"

"Turn on Channel 7 News."

"Okay, hold on. Don't hang up."

After about two minutes of silence, she spoke.

"Young? Good job boy. Now let the war begin."

"I'm ready!"

Officer Dixon

After speaking to my boss, I was more relaxed. I wasn't on his radar. Not yet anyway. My boss was up to something big, and I was gonna be the one to take his ass down. I wondered how JuJu was doing, so I gave E a call to check up on her.

"Hey E, this Ash. How are you?"

"Man I'm making it. How are you?"

"I'm living. Trying to stay above the bullshit. My boss is up to something."

"Like what?"

"I'll let you know, but it has something to do with JuJu's case. How is she anyway?"

"She not doing well right now. I had to tell her about Lil Mama's death."

"Lil Mama died? When? How?"

"Somebody cut her brakes, and then she causing her to crash after Tiki's funeral."

"Oh my poor baby. Damn I know she took that hard."

"Yeah, the guards came running from everywhere. They put

us out. Do you have anybody in there that can look out for her?"

"Actually, I have a friend that's a guard up there. After I hang up from you, I'll give her a call. I'll see if I can get her a cell phone."

"What are the odds of her being able to come to the funeral?"

"Slim, but it's worth a try. I'll hit you back in a few. Let me check on a few things."

"A'ight. Thank you, Ash."

Lil Mama died? Brakes cut? Something didn't add up. I walked over to the traffic department and found my buddy, Al.

"Hey, Al. What you up to these days?"

"Tryin' to make you my boo thang."

"Nigga, please! We like the same thing. Anyway, I need you to check something for me."

"Shoot."

"About a week and a half ago there was a bad accident. I believe the car in question is a 2014 Dodge Challenger. The cause of accident was apparently a cut brake line."

"Hold on." He typed on his computer and found what we were looking for. "Okay, there was an accident involving a pearl white Challenger and a semi-truck. The semi-truck driver was badly burned. Can you believe that?"

"So the driver of the Challenger wasn't hurt?"

"It doesn't say. The car was empty when we got there."

"She was actually smoking a cigarette at the time of the accident. I guess her hair caught fire and it quickly spread."

"One more question. What was the driver's name?"

"Ajah Heels. She was Muslim."

"Thank you, Al. I owe you."

"Well, you can..."

"Don't make me fuck you up!"

"Please!"

NINE

Chapter

Lock Jaw

Two weeks after I rushed my brother to the hospital, I brought him home with me because I didn't want no niggas trying to catch him by himself. My other lil brother was still at my crib. So far from what I know, nobody told the police who killed the dude, but I still wasn't taking any chances. I was so deep in thought that I almost missed a call from JuJu.

"Yo?"

"You have a collect call from Ja'ziya Campbell. Press 5 to accept the call."

"What's good, baby? You all right in there?"

"No I'm not. Why didn't you tell me that my auntie died?"

Damn! Who the fuck told her?

"Baby, I didn't know how to tell you some shit like that. Who told you?"

"E and ReRe came up here like two weeks ago. Why you ain't made your way up here yet?"

"Man, shit been crazy out here. My little brother got shot. I been back and forth at the hospital with him. I ain't forgot about you, love. I miss you."

I could tell that that jail shit was starting to get to her; she was so distant.

"I know you ain't forgot about me. Just get up here when you can. I chill in my cell. I don't socialize with these hoes. Will I be able to go to Lil Mama's funeral?"

"I'll have Heidi work her magic."

"One minute remaining."

"Ju, keep your head up. You'll be home in no time." *click*

Damn, that shit crazy. If I don't get her out, she's liable to snap up in that bitch. She ain't built for that shit. Out the corner of my eye, I saw Outlaw and Poohman coming into the crib.

"Poohman, where the hell y'all been?"

"I had to check on the traps, nigga. Money don't stop because nigga's get shot. We still running a business, or have you forgot?"

"You took Lil Pistol P with you I see."

"Yeah, he's bad as hell, but we need that right now. A few of our runners are getting lazy and comfortable. Your brother's just scared the shit outta Ice's ass. We need to replace them lil niggas over there in Englewood. They keep coming up short, and I can't pinpoint who's stealing. Before I kill all their asses, I'ma take the high road and replace 'em."

I thought about it for a moment. That wouldn't be a bad idea for real. Having my lil brothers would definitely save me some money.

"Aye, Money Man?"

"Huh?"

"You wanna run the spot over there on 71st and Elizabeth?"

"Hell yeah, I'm down. It's fiend city over there. Me and lil bro can make it happen."

"Don't be over there bullshitting."

"I got you, boss."

Now that that shit was settled, I called Boo to see when we

was gonna lay Lil Mama to rest.

I made sure that everything was top notch for my lil sis's funeral. It was expensive, but my boy who owns Gatlin's Funeral Home over on 101st and Halstead gave me a good ass deal. Right now, I was on my way up there to drop off her outfit. I chose this red, white, and black outfit. What? Don't ask me about shit. They were her favorite colors. The outfit was cute. I bought her some all-red Gucci pumps that I bought her for Christmas. I hated funeral homes. They always smelled like death and those cheap ass carnations. I walked towards the back of the hallway where she laid. Within every room that I passed, I couldn't help but look in at the unlucky person that occupied those caskets. Damn, life's a bitch. In the last room, there was my baby laying there as peaceful as can be. Whoever did her makeup did a damn good job, even though she was burned badly. She still looked beautiful. I was impressed. She looked like a totally different person. I pulled the sheet back to see the rest of her body. Her arms and legs were burned bad, but not the rest of her body. As a matter of fact, I could clearly see all of her tattoos.

"What the fuck?"

I looked at her chest where she was supposed to have her mother's name at. There was no name. *ring ring*

My ringing phone scared the shit outta me. I looked at the screen and saw Ashley's number.

"Hello? Hey Ash, what's up?"

"I got something I wanna tell you."

"Okay, I'm listening."

"Would it sound crazy if I told you that I don't think Lil Mama is dead?"

"Um, well maybe. How you figure that?"

"I wanted to know what she knew before I told her what I just found out. I just did a little investigation and, boo, I don't think she's dead. Can we meet?"

"Now! Meet me at Artists Lounge on 87th."

If that ain't Lil Mama, then who the fuck was she? She better be dead. Got me worrying like this. I just dropped nine stacks on this damn funeral. My boy ain't gon' give me my damn money back!

Thirty minutes later, I was sitting across from Ash with my mouth wide open. I felt a sense of relief knowing that there was a good chance that she was alive. But then I became mad as hell. Why the fuck she ain't called me yet?

"Ash, is there any way that we could find her? Her cell phone is still on because it just rings."

"I could activate her GPS app in her phone. It's worth a shot. It could take a week or two."

"Why so long?"

"Because, this is unofficial police business, meaning I'm not supposed to be doing this without permission from my higher superior. I'm doing my own investigation on him. I'm a busy girl."

TEN

Chapter

Detective Malone

"Hello?"

"What up?"

"Learn some manners when you answer the phone."

"Learn what? This my damn phone and I pay this bill. I'll answer this motha fucka the way I want to."

I swear I hate that little street punk. I had to take a deep breath. He's lucky I needed him.

"We need to meet."

"Meet for what?"

"Because the trial date is approaching fast. We need to go over a few things."

"Ain't no need for that. I know what I need to say when I get on the stand."

"Ok, what about the money?"

"How the hell should I know?"

"You better know something, damn it. I want that money that was stolen from Pancho."

"Man, that money is long gone by now. You better off getting that money that they stole from the banks."

"What banks?"

"The banks on Jeffery and Stoney. Them Eastside Crazy bitches did those robberies."

"Really?"

"I heard that they hit that bank in Hammond, Indiana, too."

That was music to my ears. The mayor was going to be pleased once I turned them little crooks in. But first, I needed to find that money.

"I really need you, Derrick. Will you help me find that money and put them away?"

"You better hope I don't kill those bitches first."

"NO, NO, NO! No more murders, damn it. I need to find that money. Don't worry about killing them. Spending the rest of their lives in jail will do the trick."

"Whatever you say."

Lil Man

That damn detective was starting to work my nerves. No more murders? What? Man, fuck that! I'm killing everybody! The whole clique has gotta go. I called a few of my cousins from out West. I told my cousins who were responsible for killing Julie and my sister. They were down to help me get them niggas. They wanted war? Well they got it now. My cousin KeeKee was the oldest. He's the trigger-happy one. His brother BayBay was the craziest. He was crazier than I was. I think he got dropped on his head a few times. No bullshit. And last but not least, there was Baby Dro. He was a year older than I was, but the nigga was certified. He got a check every month since he was two. He was the definition of a menace to society.

I really needed to see if JoJo and I were on the same page,

because if we weren't, she was going to die right along with her stanking ass sister. I was supposed to meet my cousins in the morning, so for now it was time to lay it down in the crib for the night. On my way to the crib, my vibrating phone interrupted my thoughts.

"Who the fuck is this?"

I didn't recognize the number.

"A, Lil Man, this Ice."

"Ice?"

"Man, Ice from off of Phillips. My brother, Dave, used to run with Pancho."

"Oh yeah, what up, boy? Long time no see. How you get my number?"

"I've had it nigga, but anyway I got a problem with some niggas you might know."

"Who?"

"The nigga Jaw and Poohman let me run a spot for em over there in Englewood. It's a goldmine over there. Anyway, I was their most trusted worker."

"Nigga, get to the point."

"They cut me off for no reason."

"No reason?"

"Okay, maybe I was stealing a lil bit, but so what? Their ass was bringing in over 10 G's a week."

"Jaw and Poohman, huh?"

"Yeah. I'm in my feelings. I needed that bread. Fuck them niggas. There's always money in the spot. Help me rob em."

"Let me hit you back in a few days. I might be able to help you."

Jackpot! Shit didn't get no sweeter than that. I'ma help Ice out because I can kill his ass when I finish. I ain't breaking bread with nobody. By the time I made it to the crib, I was hungry as hell. I been in them streets all day. JoJo was slacking. Lately, all she wanted to do was stay in the crib. We had shit to do. I think it was time that I reminded her ass. I walked in the crib and just as I suspected, she was in the same spot I left her ass—on the damn couch, asleep. I kicked the couch.

"Man, JoJo, get cha nasty ass up and wash yo ass or something."

"I did wash my ass and I am doing something. I'm watching T.V."

"You got a smart ass mouth. What up with that? Tell me something."

"Okay, since you all in my space, I think I'm pregnant."

"WHAT?"

"Don't act all surprised. You do fuck me without a condom even though I ask you not to."

I was stuck. I wasn't ready for no damn kid. Shit, I was still a kid my damn self. She was too. But on the other hand, when I do finally decide to have one, I might be dead.

"Come on, we 'bout to go get a test."

"Why can't you go? I don't feel good."

"Don't make this shit hard girl. You can come with me."

"Fuck it, here I come."

ReRe

"Poohman? Why the fuck is a girl named Mia calling your phone?"

"You tripping. I don't even know a girl name Mia."

"So you didn't meet her at the mall a few weeks ago?"

"Hell naw! I ain't even been to the mall. Who'd she ask for

when she called?"

"I ain't give her a chance to ask for nobody. She called like three times before I snapped on..."

"Fuck all that. I don't know that bitch. Quit fucking with my phone."

Oh yeah? Poohman gon' fuck around and pop up dead. He's lucky I knew he was telling the truth. What I really wanna know is why Jaw's got a bitch calling Poohman's phone. I'm going to see my bitch, JuJu. If Jaw think he was about to play my bestie, then he better be ready for this gunplay. I'ma put his ass to sleep before I let him hurt my girl. Poohman better stay neutral because my heart and loyalty lie with my girls for life. I love Poohman to death, but I'll kill his ass, too.

I thought my lil friend LJ was so sexy. Too bad that every time I called his phone some broad says that he's not around. I don't know what to think. For now, I'm concentrating on the demise of Lil Man, Jaw, and those Eastside Crazy bitches. I was on my way home to get JoJo's lazy ass up off my couch. We had to play catch up.

"Lil girl?"

She was lying on the couch with that creep Lil Man.

"Huh?"

"Come make a few runs with me. I'm tired of you sitting up in this house doing nothing."

I looked at Lil Man who was now mean mugging me.

"Why the fuck are you looking at me like that?"

"Because you didn't ask me if I wanted to go."

"First off, I don't have to ask you shit, little boy. I wanna spend some alone time with my sister."

"Yeah a'ight, JoJo. Tell your sister the good news."

I looked at JoJo and waiting to hear the good news.

"Well, JoJo?"

"Let me jump in the shower. I'll be ready in 30 minutes."

I was dying to know the good news, but I kept it cool because I wanted to know more about Lil Man's plans to get at Jaw.

"Mia, you know that he's planning on robbing Jaw's trap spot over on 71st and Elizabeth. That detective also wants him to break in Dirty, Jaw, and ReRe's crib looking for that bank money."

"Oh yeah?"

"Yeah, he want that money that they stole from Ramone."

"You're not doing that shit with him. Revenge is one thing, but breaking into other people's shit is stupid. I got money. Fuck that. Here's what we're going to do. I'ma call Jaw and let him know that Lil Man is planning on breaking in his shit and robbing his spot. Let him handle him. Less work for us."

"We can kill Dirty and that green-eyed bitch, ReRe."

"JoJo, you ain't never killed nobody. Let me take care of that. What's the good news?"

I could tell that the news wasn't good to her.

"I'm pregnant."

"JoJo, noooo. Damn it! I thought I told you to wear condoms. I can't believe you let that lil dirty ass boy nut in you. You are getting an abortion."

"Actually Mia, I wanna keep my baby."

I could have died.

"Fuck No! I don't wanna have to put up with that crazy ass nigga for 18 years. JoJo think; do you really wanna deal with Lil Man for that long?"

"He's going to die, so I won't have to."

"I'm not helping you take care of that demon's child."

"That's not fair."

"Fuck fair, you're on your own with that one. End of discussion."

I was mad as hell. I ain't care what she talking about. She wasn't keeping that baby.

"Where my phone JoJo? Never mind."

I was thinking about how I was gonna tell Jaw that Lil Man was planning on robbing him.

"Yo? Who is this calling me private?"

"You ask too many questions. Lil Man is planning on robbing that spot you got in Englewood."

"What spot in Englewood? Who the fuck is this?"

"I warned you. You better stay on point."

"Is that right? You should tell me who you are, so I can take you out for looking out for me."

"I'll pass!" *click*

ELEVEN

Chapter

JuJu

I never thought in a million years that I would be spending Christmas in jail. I felt as if I was going to suffocate. I never came out of my room. I didn't wanna interact with them hoes. The one day that I decided that I was gonna make the best of my situation, all hell broke loose. I had just come back from an attorney visit. He told me that the state's witness was in fact Lil Man. I mean, really? I needed to see Jaw so I could tell him to go find that motha fucka before my trial date. I came back to the unit and headed straight for the phones. There was a line, so I patiently waited. Well, while I was waiting, four girls walked passed me mean mugging me. I shook my head and closed my eyes trying to calm my nerves. I needed to calm the beast inside of me that was dying to come out. When I opened my eyes, the four girls were now standing in front of me. Y'all know this is the kind of shit I live for. Ain't no hoe in me. I was the first one to speak.

"What's good?"

The short dark-skinned girl with a terrible weave walked up to me and got a lil bit too close for my liking.

"What you mean what's good? What do you say when I

walked pass you?"

"What you think I said?"

"You called me a 'bitch.'"

I had to laugh to hide the anger that was spewing out of me.

"I don't even know you to even say anything to you, but fuck all that. What's crackin?"

I wasn't doing anymore talking. I took a step back and got into my beat-a-hoe-down stance. I guess the ugly bitch was shocked at how I came at her. She probably thought I was gonna tuck my tail or something. But I wasn't that kinda girl; and just to show them that I wasn't, I took off on her ass first. *WHAM* I punched her dead in her throat. She didn't fall, so I quickly followed up with a kick to the gut. *BOOM* I was a bit worried about the other three bitches jumping in, so I made sure that the one I was fighting got it the worse. After hitting her with a three-piece combo, we fell to the ground together. Two of the three girls stepped in to help their friend. I wasn't about to let 'em stomp me out. I jumped up and hit the first one that came after me. *BOOP* That one went flying back into her friend. I rushed 'em both and dropkicked the one that fell on her friend in the stomach, sending both of them flying to the ground.

"Y'all bitches got me fucked up."

I was in a zone now. I needed to let it be known that just because I was quiet, I wasn't nobody's punk. The bitch I hit first jumped on my back.

"Bitch, get the fuck off my back."

I backed up to the wall and slammed her against it. After I rammed her back into the wall multiple times, she tried to stick her nails into my face. I couldn't let her scratch my pretty face. I peeled her hand and bent her fingers so far back that I heard a cracking noise.

She screamed, "OUUCCHH!"

"Get the fuck off of my back, bitch!"

Shit, I was beginning to get tired. I didn't know how much longer I was going to last.

"BREAK IT UP!"

Saved by the bell. The C.O. walked into the unit with a Taser gun. She looked mad as fuck. I was glad I got my rocks off because I knew for a fact that I was going to the SHU.

"Jones, Brown, and Sanders? Get the fuck on the wall NOW!"

She turned to look at me and smiled. "I see you can hold your own."

"I wasn't about to let them beat my ass."

"I saw the whole thing. I should lock your ass up too, but I'm not. Let that be the last time you disrupt my unit."

"Yes ma'am."

She stepped closer to me.

"You are on room restriction for five days."

I was cool with that. She came even closer. She was so close that I could smell her Double Mint gum.

"I put a phone under your pillow."

I was stuck. "Huh?"

"Ashley said to call her."

After that, she took the other three girls I fought to the SHU. I walked back to my room when the fourth girl that was with the group called me.

"Hey Ju? Let me holler at you."

"Bitch, look, I'm tired. You should have fought me when I fought them. I'ma cut your fucking face if you run up on me."

"Naw, it ain't even like that. I was never gonna help them jump you. I just heard that you get down. I wanted to see how you handled yourself."

63

"Who the fuck are you?"

"My name's Jade. I'm from over East, too."

"How you know me though?"

"Everybody know about y'all. Sorry to hear about Tiki."

Who was this girl? I wasn't about to let my guard down. I didn't know this hoe.

"Where you from over East?"

"You really don't remember me, do you? I used to live next door to you when you stayed on 88th and Marquette. I moved after my dad killed my mother and himself."

"Damn, I do remember you. We went to Phil Sheridan together."

I didn't know her to trust her, but it was nice to have someone I knew from home. I really needed to call Jaw, so I told her that I would get at her later. I hopped in my bed and grabbed the phone that was under my pillow. *Thank you, Ash.*

I dialed Jaw's number. "Hello?" Who the fuck was this bitch answering my man's phone.

"Who the fuck are you, and why are you answering my man's phone?"

Jaw

"You better stay on point, boy. If y'all see anything that don't look right, start shooting."

Ever since I got the call that Lil Man was planning on robbing my spot, I had been on full alert. How the fuck did he even know that I had a spot over here? I made the most money over here. Killing Big T was the best move we could have ever made. The hood accepted us and allowed us eat. I walked to the front room, and looked at my lil brother, Money Man, save a few friends.

64

"Ain't no $8 bags, nigga. If you want this shit, come with all my money or don't come at all."

"Aw, come on young blood, hook me up."

"NEXT!"

I laughed because that nigga was a fool.

"Money Man, I'm about to break out and check on the other spots. I'll be back."

I jumped in my car and hit the streets. I was missing my girl; I still haven't took my ass up there to see her yet. Yeah, I know I was bogus. That visit might break her down. Shit me too! I pulled over because I saw a familiar face.

"What's good, stranger?"

"What's up, parking spot thief."

I must admit shorty was looking all right in all-white STRUT jeans with knee-high Timbs. Her Pelle Pelle was cute as shit, too. Even her micros were fresh.

"What's crackin', girl?"

"Apparently nothing, since you gave me your friend's number instead of yours."

"I know, that was my bad. Take my number."

I felt guilty for giving her my number, but I wasn't doing shit wrong. I just needed a friend to talk to. Nothing was going to make me mess up what I got going on with Ju. I loved her to death.

"So LJ, what brings you outside in the cold?"

"I was running around checking on a few spots."

"Spots? You serve?"

"I do me. Why?"

"Shit! Maybe we can get some money together."

"Get in, ma. It's cold as shit out here. Where your car?"

"On the block, why?"

"Hit some blocks with me."

We rode around and talked for hours. Shorty was cool as fuck. I learned that her brothers and cousin had all been murdered, and she was taking care of her little sister. I felt bad for her. I didn't really tell her none of my business. She was cool but I ain't know her like that.

"Ma, you hungry?"

She smiled and shook her head.

"Well what you want?"

"I want some Wendy's."

I shot up to Wendy's on 87th and Stoney Island.

"What you want?"

"A number 3 and a pink lemonade."

This nigga was fine and about his business. I had to make him mine. He didn't said anything about having a girl, so that was a good thing. I couldn't believe how open I was with him about my brothers and my cousin. I didn't say their names because my family was into everything in this city. Chicago's real small. They might have done something to him or somebody he knew. He was a great listener, and I needed that. I had so many things on my mind. How was I going to kill Jaw and those Eastside bitches? I needed JoJo to abort that damn demon child she was carrying. I had to figure out a way to get Lil Man outta our lives. Yep, I had a full plate. Did I even want this man to distract me from reality? *ring ring* I heard his phone ringing. Normally I wouldn't have answered it; but since we were into the same business, I knew he wouldn't have minded. It might be about some money.

"Hello?"

"Who the fuck is this, and why are you answering my man's phone?"

Aw, shit! So much for him not having a girlfriend.

Boo

It had been two weeks since I'd heard from Ashley. I was dying to know if she traced Lil Mama's phone. My boy didn't give me my damn money back, so I buried a stranger. I had been so concerned with the whole Lil Mama situation that I hadn't notice until now that my pockets were slimming down. It took Heidi to put me back on point. She came busting through my door looking like the Grinch who stole Christmas. She had on a lime green jumpsuit with some knee-high boots on and a big ass fur.

"For real bitch?"

"What?"

"Where are you going looking like a big ass apple jolly rancher?"

"You a hater! This is Roberto Cavalli, and it's fresh off the runway."

"Whatever! Where you going?"

"Get dressed. It's Christmas Eve. We're going to this party downtown."

"Naw, I'm not in the mood. Ju in jail, Lil Mama's missing, and Tiki's dead. It's just all too much for me."

She stared at me as if I was crazy.

"Boo, Lil Mama's dead. Let's move on, baby."

I hadn't even told her what Ashley and I had been working on. Now was the perfect time.

"Sit down."

After about 30 minutes and a few outbursts, I was able to get out the whole story.

"That lil bony bitch. I'ma kick her ass. Got us worried like this."

Heidi was fuming.

"Chill, Heidi! There's a reason why she disappeared. I just gotta wait for her to get at me."

I thought for a few seconds, and then it hit me.

"She had cameras on her car, Heidi. We need to get to the tow yard."

"Bitch, it's cold as hell out there; and as you can see, I'm rocking this new shit. I'm not going to no damn tow yard."

"Yes you are. You better change. I know you gotcha hoe bag in your trunk. Now hurry up."

Thirty minutes later, we were at the pound looking at her mangled car, if she did in fact survive that crash. I know she fucked up. Her car was totaled. While I was looking through her car, I saw Heidi out of the corner of my eye stomping her feet as if she had an attitude.

"How are we gonna get the camera footage now, genius?"

I was about to curse her ass out when I saw a button to the trunk that spelled camera. When I pushed the button, a small SB chip popped out.

"Now can we go? Bitch, I'm freezing."

"Man, ain't nobody tell you to put on them thin ass leggings with that little ass T-shirt."

"This this is my morning-after gear."

"Morning after what? Let's go!"

I was dying to see what was on that chip. We grabbed something to eat and headed back to my crib. I didn't know what to expect. Shit, Heidi was more anxious than I was. There was so much footage on that chip. We sat there for hours. Lil Mama was watching the police detective; often!

"Heidi, why the hell was she following him like that?"

I was so confused. The detective dude had even met with Lil Man a few times.

"Heidi, something ain't right."

Finally, we were at the day of Tiki's funeral.

"Okay, Heidi look. This is where she left the funeral in a hurry. Look at the camera's view. She's swerving. This must be when she was on the phone with me. Oh God."

The dash cam showed Lil Mama swerve into oncoming traffic. We saw a big ass ball of fire. The car even flipped a few times. All that and the camera was still rolling.

Heidi jumped up, and said, "PAUSE IT RIGHT THERE!"

"Damn bitch, you scared the shit outta me. Why you yell like that? What you see?"

"Unpause it and look at the figure running towards the car."

When I unpaused it, I saw a familiar face running towards the car. Three seconds later, I saw that same person dragging Lil Mama's limp body from the car. I was shocked.

"I can't believe this shit. Heidi, hand me my phone."

I've been riding around solo. I missed my dawg. Tiki was my ace boon coon. I woke up today as if it was just a regular day. In all actuality, it was Christmas. I'm not going to lie, I cried like a baby. I was so lost. I knew that I was going to murder that bastard. I just couldn't catch his ass. It was a long shot, but I called the one person that knew where he was.

"Hello?"

"You lucky I didn't kill you bitch. My bestie died because of you and that nigga. Tell me why I shouldn't kill you."

It was quiet on the other end for several seconds. For a moment, I thought I had fucked up by going so hard.

"It wasn't my fault that Tiki died."

"Do you know that he just shot at me, Re, and Poohman?"

"No, I ain't know that, E. I can't talk on this phone. If you agree not to hurt me, I'll help you get him."

"Why should I believe you? Remember you were trying to have me killed?"

"Correction, I was going to kill you myself."

I had to pull the phone away from my ear and look at it. The nerve of that hoe.

"Yo, you got balls for real."

"It ain't that, E, it's the truth. I don't expect you to sympathize with me. Y'all killed my brothers and my cousin."

She was talking reckless on this phone. For all I know, she was recording the call to try and set me up.

"I ain't kill nobody. If you gon' meet me, pick the spot and be there. I need to talk to you."

"Meet me at Jackson Park Hospital."

"Why there?"

"I got a doctor's appointment."

"What time?"

"1:30 p.m."

"Bye."

I needed her to lead me to Lil Man. After she served her purpose, I was going to kill her ass as well.

Twenty minutes later, I was sitting in my car in the hospital parking lot. I really didn't think that she was going to show up. I was about to pull off when I saw her walking towards my car. I popped the locks so she could get in. I started laughing because she made no effort to even touch the door. Smart girl! I zipped my Pelle up and hopped out. I ain't even gon' lie, seeing her again was like a breath of fresh air. She was glowing.

"Merry Christmas, E."

"Fuck you, JoJo."

"You were the one trying to kill me."

"How you gon' plot against me with that nigga, Lil Man?"

"I didn't know you first. Let's get that out of the way. I just wanted to find out what happened to my family, and then things got outta control. I had nothing to do with Tiki dying."

I believed her, but so what. She was gonna die.

"So, perhaps all of that is true. Why are you still around that nigga? He's going to die. If I can help it, it's going to be painful."

She put her head down, and I could sense that this wasn't gonna end well for her.

"E, I'm pregnant."

"It ain't mine."

I had to laugh at that shit. That shit was funny.

"For real, it's Lil Man's."

"You gave that dirty ass nigga some pussy?"

"It wasn't even like that. He sort of takes what he wants."

"Damn, What you gon' do?"

"Find a way for him to die, and keep my baby."

"Maybe I could help you with that, but I need you to help me get him."

"I know how you get down E. I'll help you, but I don't wanna die. I bit off more than I could chew dealing with him. I just wanna take my baby and move away."

The more I stood there and listened to her, the more I actually felt sorry for her. Lil Man fucked my life up by killing my friend. If I could choose as to who I wanted more, it would be him.

"JoJo, what he planning?"

"He called his cousins from out west to help him. They planning on robbing Jaw's trap spot in Englewood."

"Oh yeah?"

"He was the one that called Crime Stoppers and told them that JuJu was the one that killed Tae and Tiki."

"Anything else?"

"Watch your back. That detective dude wants the money that y'all stole from Pancho. He told Lil Man to hit y'all cribs and look for that money."

Damn, I didn't think that Lil Man would try and go that hard. I gotta get up with Young and ReRe.

"A'ight JoJo. I'ma check into this shit. If you're lying, I'm telling you now that I'm going to kill you and that bastard you carrying."

"Oh, I'm not lying; but if anybody wanna come after me because of Lil Man, I'ma change their minds. I'm trying to survive."

"I hope you do!"

THIRTEEN | *Chapter*

Young Meech

I had to get a handle on myself. Today was a bad day for me. It's Christmas. My auntie, Tiki, and my girl were all dead. I wanted all of this to be a dream. After killing Lil Man's people, I felt nothing. I won't feel any better until I put that nigga in the ground. I didn't ask for this life. Now it seems as if there's no way out. I had big shoes to fill from the very beginning. My heart was so cold. Man, I'm only 15. I never wanted to be a kingpin. I really wanted to be a ball player. But that was then and this is now. I was going to torture and bury Lil Man and everybody that he loved. *cough cough*

"You a'ight? Drink this water."

"Thank you, baby."

"You look better."

"I feel better."

"So what's the plan?"

"Detective Malone is going to do his best to try and bury Ju, Re, and Dirty. We just have to get to him first."

"We? Do you know what you're saying? We are about to go after a cop?"

"If we don't, they're going to spend the rest of their lives behind bars. I'm not going to let that happen."

"Why not call ...?"

"No! Boo is already under his radar for killing A. We're going to do this together; and then after that, you can go get Lil Man. Without them two, the state has no case."

Well then, we needed to handle this as soon as possible because Lil Man's ass is mine.

"When you gon' call Boo?"

"Together we are easy targets. After I eliminate the problem, we can go back to doing us."

"She is going to kill me when she finds out I have you with me."

"You are right about that."

Lil Man

Christmas Night

"KeeKee, y'all ready to do that thang?"

"Nigga, which thang? You said tonight that we were breaking into cribs and robbing trap spots."

"We are doing it all. First we're gon' hit the trap spot. After we get in there, shoot everything living. We are taking money and work. You guys can have all the drugs. I want the money."

Baby Dro spoke up: "Hell naw. Why do you get all the money?"

"Because y'all sell drugs, dummy. I got a baby on the way. I need the money like right now."

I guess I said something that was funny because KeeKee started cracking up.

"Nigga, who gave you some pussy? You still wet behind the

ears."

"Nigga, I'm grown. My dick spits, so fuck you!"

We needed to begin moving before those niggas made me mad.

"At 11:00 p.m. we are gon' hit the spot. Let me call my girl and check on her before we roll out."

All three of my cousins burst out laughing. What the fuck was funny? This was going to be a long night.

Jaw

"Money Man, I'ma come over there and let you off for the night."

"I'm cool. I got weed, my bitch, and my gun. Merry Christmas. Why don't you shoot up to the county and see your girl?"

"Damn, you right. I'm slipping. Come to think about it, she ain't called me in like a week. I'll holla at y'all when I get there."

Just as I was about to leave, I saw Outlaw bobbing up the street on his way back to the spot.

"Where have you been?"

"I went to the liquor store to grab something to drink, but fuck all that. Check this out. How come that nigga, Ice who you had running the spot around here is now talking about sticking up the spot?"

I was kind of surprised. Here I was giving the nigga a pass for stealing. Now he wants to rob us? Wait 'til I tell Poohman this shit.

"A'ight, look, be on point. Money Man, send your girl home. This ain't no place for her right now."

She quickly spoke up, "Um, Jaw, no offense, but I'm not just some pretty face."

She went into her book bag and pulled out this big ass gun.

"I know how to make this thang talk." *Click Clack*

"We ready. Let them niggas come!"

Man, Joe, she cocked that motha fucker like a pro.

"Damn shorty, I see you. Money Man, where you get her from?"

He just smiled.

"Yeah bro, she's my rider. Let them niggas come. We gon' bring the 4th of July to December."

This shit was about to get real. If that's what Ice was really on, then his ass wasn't 'bout to make it to the New Year!

"Let me go see my girl real quick. I'm bringing Poohman and Young Meech back with me."

Money Man looked puzzled.

"Young Meech? Is he kin to King Meech?"

"Yup."

"Aw, hell yeah. Let's get it. Anybody who's thinking about running up in here must really wanna die. Let's help 'em."

FOURTEEN

Chapter

Ju Ju

Throughout the previous week, I was sick to my stomach. Some girl answered my man's phone. I was so hurt I couldn't even call back. The crazy part about it was that the girl that answered the phone said that I was going to be replaced. She was lucky that I couldn't get to her. I called the one person that I knew could get to the bottom of this.

"Hello? Who is this?"

"This me, Re."

"Ju? You out? Whose phone you got?"

"Ashley's friend gave it to me."

"Oh, that's cool. How you been, boo?"

"I've seen better days. I beat a few hoes up for trying me."

"That's my girl. You don't sound right. What's really good?"

I forgot how well she knew me. I debated on telling her the problem. Re was crazy. Things could go left really quick. If I tell her that Jaw was cheating, she was liable to hurt that boy. Oh well, he did it to himself.

"I called Jaw's phone and some bitch answered the phone. She told me I was being replaced."

"Her name is Mia."

I was stuck. How the hell did she know?

"Re, you knew?"

"A few weeks ago some girl started calling Poohman's phone looking for LJ. I grilled Poohman about it. He said he didn't know what the fuck I was talking about."

"Who is the bitch then?"

"A dead one!"

I heard the officer calling my name.

"Re, let me hit you back, The C.O. is calling me."

"Okay, love you."

"Love you, too."

I went to the officer's station and I was notified that I had a visitor. Who could it be? I fixed my hair and then I was escorted to the visiting room. My visitor hadn't made it yet, so I found a booth all the way in the corner. About five minutes later, here comes this nigga Jaw walking in. When he saw me, he had the nerve to smile.

"Bitch ass nigga."

Jaw

I hated coming up here man. These slow ass guards take all day to get you in. After like an hour and a half, I was walking through the door to the visiting room. I saw my girl sitting in the last booth. I couldn't help but to smile when I saw her. Shit, but the look that I got back wiped that smile right off of my face. I grabbed the phone and waited for her to pick it up. After about 10 seconds, she finally snatched the phone up.

"Damn, ma, why you staring at me like you wanna kill me?

What I do?"

"Since when did you start letting bitches answer your phone?"

"Answer my phone? Girl, ain't nobody other than me been answering my phone."

I could tell that she wasn't trying to hear that shit.

"You lying! The bitch told me that I was going to be replaced. Tell me who the fuck she is."

"Man, shorty, I ain't been around no bitches. You tripping. You my girl and I love you. Ain't no replacing you."

It broke my heart because she started to cry.

"You gon' pay for doing me like this. I gave you my heart, my body, and my love. I hope she was worth it."

She got up, hocked up some spit, and then spit on the glass directly where my face was. If this glass weren't here, I would have been in jail for killing her ass right then. Still holding the phone, I was shocked.

"Damn shorty, that's how you feel?"

She gave me the look of death; and just like that, she was gone. Who the fuck has she been talking to? That whole little scene just fucked my head up. I got up and left that building as fast as I could. I needed a drink. I shot up California and made a left on 71st. I was headed to the liquor store on Western. It was juking out there tonight. I hopped outta the car and headed to the store with one thing on my mind ... REMY!

"Damn, stranger, you following me?"

I turned around to see Mia's sexy ass standing there looking very fuckable.

"What up girl? Merry Christmas."

"Same to you. Why you ain't called me?"

"You know how it is. I've been hella busy. Why are you not at home enjoying a nice dinner?"

"Because you ain't cook it."

"Okay that was cute. What you on right now? You wanna roll with me then?"

"Yeah, let me tell my girls to keep my car. Get me some Patron."

After I paid for our drinks, I walked back to my car and waited for her. *ring ring*

"Yo?"

"Bruh, this Money Man. Where you at?"

"At the liquor store. I'm on the way."

"Bring me some cigars. I got this LOUD I'm trying to blow."

"I'll be there in like five minutes. Anything happened yet?"

"Besides, Outlaw knocking out Fred the crackhead, nope."

"Why'd he knock him out?"

"Because he came with $6."

I started laughing. My lil brothers were wild as shit. Finally, after around 10 minutes, the ole girl jumped in.

"Damn, it took yo ass forever."

"Where we going?"

"To chill."

I hoped tonight was going to be a peaceful one. I had a gut feeling that I was going to be wrong.

ReRe

"Come on, Re, visiting hours are about to be over."

"All right Bay, I'm coming."

You know I had to go see my girl for Christmas. I knew she was going through it. Hell, we all were. It wasn't crowed when we got there. Thank God. When my bestie walked in, her eyes were bloodshot red. That shit was hard to look at. I tried to smile but I couldn't. There wasn't no need to pretend. I was the first one to speak.

"Hey Ju, fix your fucking face. Don't let them bitches see you like this."

"Man, fuck these hoes. I've done already let it be known that I'm 'bout my business. I got hands and they know it. Ain't shit sweet over here? I'm crying because Jaw just left from up here."

"It's okay."

"I just cursed his ass out. I asked him about ole girl, and he swears up and down that ain't let no bitch touched his phone."

"Don't worry about it. I said I'ma look into that shit. No stress. I got you. You just need to focus on winning this case, so you can come home. We can find you another man."

She started crying even harder.

"I don't want another man. I want him, Re."

"You can want him all you want. But if he's cheating on you, I'ma kill his ass."

"I love you. I'ma call you later. Please let me know something."

"Don't worry."

I kissed my hand and put it up to the glass. She did the same and walked off. Poohman had nothing to do with this. He has been so good to me. I would hate to have to kill him, too. I never really knew what love was 'til I met his crazy ass. He was everything to me. Lord, please let everything be okay. When we made it back to the car, he handed me the keys.

"It's your turn to drive."

I just smiled because, well, damn I love this man.

"Lazy ass. Where am I driving us to?"

"We 'bout to go fuck with Jaw for a minute at the trap. I heard it might be some trouble."

"Trouble? You know I got them thangs in the trunk?"

"I know G.I Jane. That's why you are going with me. You want something to smoke on?"

"Yeah. I'm 'bout to call Dirty and tell her to meet us over there. She just bought a new toy."

"Yo, what up maniac?"

"I got yo maniac pussy. What you doing?"

"Over here juicing JoJo outta information."

"JOJO?"

"Calm down killa. She's been telling me all about Lil Man and some other shit."

"Man, I don't like that shit. You just need to murk that slut and be done with it."

"You're so quick to kill somebody. Damn, let me handle this. What did you call me for?"

"We 'bout to hit the spot in Englewood. There might be some gunplay. You wanna party?"

"Hell yeah, I'm game. I'm going to bring shorty, so be nice."

"Yeah a'ight. You better hope that hoe don't accidently catch a bullet." *click*

My bestie needed some help. I could kill two birds with one stone.

"JoJo, wanna come chill at the spot with me?"

She whipped her head around so fast that I thought for sure that her big ass head was going to fall off.

"Um, are you talking about the same spot that Lil Man and his cousins are trying to rob tonight?"

"That's the one."

"Absolutely not! I'm not trying to die tonight. I'm actually looking forward to being a mother."

I just shook my head.

"I can't believe you are gon' keep that nigga's baby."

"I can't change who I got pregnant by. It's my baby. Can we change the subject?"

"Fuck it, I'ma drop you off at home."

Her phone started ringing, so I grabbed it off the table to see who was calling her. Well I'll be damned. It was him.

"E, don't."

She snatched the phone right before I hit talk.

"Hey. I'm at the library. I'm about to go home now. Bye."

"What did he say?"

"You might wanna get over there to your friends, because they are about to make their move."

I looked at my watch. It was almost 10:00 p.m.

"Come on, let me take you home."

"Naw, you need to get there. I can take a cab. Be careful."

FIFTEEN

Chapter

Boo

After I saw who took Lil Mama, I was furious. I mean, why not take her, and then call us? She looked as if she was in bad shape. I needed to see Ashley. She was going to trip out when I tell her this shit.

"Hi, you've reached Ashley. Leave a message."

"Call me, it's Boo, and it's important."

I was a little worried. I hadn't heard from her in almost three weeks. That's not like her. Now I had to get my Sherlock Holmes on and go find Ms. Ashley. I hoped her boss didn't find out that she was helping us. I called the only person I knew that was willing to get on some gangsta shit ... Heidi!

"Sis? What you doing?"

"I'm 'bout to jump on some good ole holiday dick. What you want?"

"I need you. I think something happened to Ashley."

"Well gah-damn! These bitches don't know how to watch they backs? I mean we is in Chicago aka CHI-raq. Wait a minute. Are you sure? You know how paranoid yo ass can get."

"Fuck you bitch. I ain't never paranoid. Careful is more up my alley, and yes I'm sure. I haven't heard from her since she said she was investigating her boss. I also know that her boss got it out for JuJu and them other bad ass kids."

"I got that impression when I went up there to see JuJu. So what do you wanna do?"

"I think we need to go over to Tiki and E's crib, and snoop through some of Ashley's shit. She has still been staying there. I need to know what she found out."

"So in other words, we are about to go break in to those people's house?"

"Yep."

"Let me get my nut off then; because fucking with you, we gon' go to jail for breaking and entering."

"Be there in thirty minutes."

"Thirty minutes? Bitch I'ma freak. I'll get to your house when I'm done."

Two hours later. *knock knock*

Who the hell was knocking at my door at 10 after midnight? I grabbed my gun and stood on the side of the door.

"Who is it?"

"Heidi."

I opened the door and started cracking up.

"What the fuck so funny?"

The lady had a terrible sense of fashion. At 12:00 a.m., she was standing in my living room wearing a one-piece pajama onesie, some black Tims, and a big ass Northface.

"Why the fuck you got that damn onesie on?"

"Fuck you, I'm comfortable."

"I know. I got one, too. Let's get down to business. We are looking for anything that could tell us anything about Detective Malone. Apparently, Lil Mama found something out because she was watching him, as well."

"I'm strapped this time."

"Where did yo scary ass get a gun from?"

"Don't worry about all that. I got connections. I'm not 'bout to be caught slipping."

"Calm yo crazy ass down, so we can get this shit over with."

Young Meech

Tonight I was hitting the streets. I was hungry as hell, but I didn't want food. I wanted blood! I was doing my best to nurse my houseguest back to health. Things were about to get real crazy. I had to hurry up and find Lil Man. I couldn't sleep. He was in my dreams. I wanted that nigga so bad I could taste his blood. I needed some action in my life. I knew just who to call.

"Hello?"

"Dirty, what's good?"

"Young, what up? I was just about to call you."

"Shit, I need to get out and get some fresh air. What's cracking for tonight?"

"You ain't gon' believe this shit."

"Try me."

"Lil Man and his cousins supposed to be tryin' to hit Jaw's trap spot tonight."

My adrenaline started pumping. My palms started sweating. I needed to be there.

"Man, I'm on my way."

Lil Man

Tonight I was going to make my move, but I heard that Ice's

stupid ass was running his mouth about what we had planned to do. I knew that tonight wasn't the right time. I bet my life that the block was on lockdown. It still worked out in my favor; because now I was just gonna hit Dirty and Jaw's crib.

"BayBay get ready and put that weed out. You have been smoking all day. Yo ass might forget what you are supposed to be doing when we get there. Be on point."

"Man, shut yo young ass up. Nigga I do this."

"Yeah a'ight. We are looking for money, safes, and anything else that we might wanna take." Baby Dro smiled.

"I'm getting all the dope."

"Fine by me. The money we find is not for us. It's going to a very important person."

I had to lie. I couldn't let them know that I was working with the police. They would have fucked me up. BayBay shook his head.

"We better be getting paid since we are looking for something for the next nigga."

"BayBay, I'ma pay y'all. I shouldn't have to because I know its gon' be some shit in there y'all gon' like."

Ole thirsty ass niggas. That's why I didn't fuck with 'em like that. We hit Dirty and Tiki's crib since they lived around the corner.

It took us forever to find a parking spot. These people around here are serious about their parking spots. Motha fuckers got chairs in the street reserving their spots. Who does that?"

"Ok Heidi, you go up the front stairs. I'ma hit the back."

"Why can't we go together? E ain't home."

"How you know?"

"She with Jaw are in Englewood. Lil Man was supposed to be trying to rob the spot. All my boys over there."

After we made our way upstairs, I picked the lock and made my way to Tiki's room. I felt kinda funny for going through her things. Ashley had some of her things over here, so I went through her shit.

"Come here, Heidi. Look at what Ashley wrote about her boss. It's like a journal."

Detective Malone was quite a character. He really did have it out for JuJu.

"Girl, Lil Man is the eyewitness in their case."

"Shit, I'm trying to figure out why Ashley had this thing lying around like that!"

"Maybe he was on to her, Boo. That's why she had the book over here."

Heidi had a point.

"We need to hit Ashley's crib next."

After putting everything back where we found it, we were on our way to the front door when I heard the door jiggle. Heidi grabbed me and whispered.

"Bitch, that's the police. We are going to jail."

I snatched away from her when I heard the familiar sound of a pistol being cocked. *Click Clack*

"Bitch, that ain't the police. Where is yo gun at?"

Them niggas thought I was gonna hit the spot. I was two steps ahead of their dumb asses.

"A'ight, me and KeeKee are gon' hit the crib. BayBay and Baby Dro, y'all keep watch in the gangway."

"BayBay shook his head.

"Nope, fuck that. We don't do it like that out West. We all go in or nothing. You ain't running the show."

That nigga was lucky he was my cousin.

"All right then, lead the way BayBay. "

I was the first one to hit the stairs because I knew which apartment it was.

"This is the one. Get ready."

Click Clack I gave KeeKee a dirty ass look.

"Nigga, you should have already had one in the chamber. That was loud as shit."

I checked the doorknob. To my surprise, it was unlocked. Baby Dro wanted to be the first one in, so he pushed past me.

"Nigga wait!"

Next thing I heard was "Yeah nigga ... surprise."

Heidi

I gave my gun to Boo because her aim was a lot better than mine was. She was on one side of the door, and I stood on the other side. When the door opened, I saw this lil nigga trying to rush in on us.

"Yeah nigga ... surprise." *WHAM* I hit that lil nigga so hard he started snoring before he even hit the ground.

"Boo, let's run. Head for the back door."

We took off running towards the back door. I turned around to see the devil himself running through the front door.

"Boo, shoot him." I didn't have to tell her twice. *BOC, BOC,*

BOC, BOC
"FUCK!"

I was out through the back door and down the stairs before I knew it. Boo was about five steps behind me.

"Heidi, go get the car!"

"Get the car? Bitch you better come on."

She seemed like she was slowing down. I didn't have time to stop. I needed to get to that car or our asses were grass. *BOC BOC*

"Boo, come on."

I made it to the car and pulled up to the gangway. Boo was nowhere in sight.

"Come on, sis, where are you at?"

After Heidi gave me her gun, I was ready. I refused to get shot again. The door came flying open and in ran this little punk. Before I could blink, Heidi hit that boy so hard he fell asleep in the air. "Damn."

"Boo let's run. Head for the back door."

Shit, Heidi hauled ass out of the back door. I was right behind her. I turned around to see Lil Man hot on our asses.

"Boo, shoot him." *BOC, BOC, BOC, BOC*

"Fuck!" he screamed!

I thought I hit him until I saw him flying down the stairs behind me. I wasn't about to let him catch me. When I got to the bottom of the stairs, I let off two more shots. *BOC, BOC* I heard Heidi scream.

"Boo come on."

She ran through the gangway and I hit the alley. It was hard running in the snow, but I had no choice. Run or Die! I didn't see

Lil Man behind me, so I dipped through a gangway to look for Heidi. When I saw her creeping up the street, I ran to the car to get in.

"Bitch, unlock the door!

When she did, I jumped in and screamed, "PULL OFF!"

I immediately called Dirty.

"Yo, what's up, Boo?"

"LIL MAN IN YO CRIB"

I was outta breath, tired and cold.

"In my crib?"

"Yes. Just get there. He's not alone. Bring somebody with you."

I hung up the phone and put my head back.

"Heidi, you think they followed us over there?"

"I don't think so, but damn that was close."

"We need to find Ashley. Something ain't right."

"You're damn right something ain't right. Every time I'm with you, we end up running for our lives. This shit has got to stop. After we find Ashley and get to the bottom of things, I'm done."

I looked at her and laughed.

"What, you scared? Not tough ass Heidi."

"Fuck you, I am tough."

"You scared?"

"Hell yeah!"

Dirty E

By the time I made it to Jaw's spot, it was a shortly after midnight. There were people everywhere. Lil Man didn't know what we had in store for his ass tonight. He was going to die, and I hoped it was going to be by the hands of me.

"E, come here. Let me holler at you."

I walked over to where he stood, and I was a bit on the confused side. Why was that bitch Mia there, and what the fuck was she doing with Jaw?

"What's good, Dirty? You a'ight?"

"Yeah I'm good. What's up with you?"

I eyed Mia, and he motioned for me to walk off with him.

"It ain't even like that. Shorty cool, E. We are doing some business together."

I just shook my head. See that's why I'm glad I'm gay. Niggas be out here thinking with their dirty ass dicks.

"I ain't said shit. You are grown, but if my bestie asks me, you know I'm going to tell her."

"I respect that, but ain't shit going on."

"I'm cool. You cool Jaw?"

"In that order."

I walked off to mingle with some cats I knew when my phone rang. It was Young.

"Hello?"

"Dirty, what's good?"

"Young, what up? I was just about to call you."

"Shit, I need to get out and get some fresh air. What's cracking for tonight?"

"You ain't gon' believe this shit."

"Try me."

"Lil Man and his cousins are supposed to be hitting Jaw's trap spot tonight."

"Man, I'm on my way."

No sooner than I hung up, I saw ReRe and Poohman walk through the door. When I locked eyes on ReRe, she was looking dead at Jaw and Mia.

"Aw shit."

I knew that Lil Man wasn't the only person we needed to worry about tonight.

"E, who is that bitch over there with Jaw? Is that Mia?"

I was shocked that she even knew her. I never told nobody her name.

"How you know Mia?"

"I don't but she was calling Poohman's phone asking for LJ. She even answered Jaw's phone when Ju called."

"You bullshitting?"

"You wish. How do you know her?"

I gave her my 'wouldn't you like to know' smile.

"She's JoJo's sister."

Her mouth hung open for a few minutes before I closed it.

"So that dummy is sleeping with the devil, and he don't even know it."

"Nope."

"Good. Don't tell him. I'm gonna kill em both."

Damn, my bestie was harsh.

"You can whack that bitch, but leave Jaw alone."

"What the fuck you mean leave Jaw alone? He betrayed Ju. He's going to die."

"He might die, but not by the hands of you. If you kill him, we gotta face Boo. I don't want to go to war with that lady."

Re was tripping.

"Boo ain't gon' let that shit ride. You know that woman's reach is long."

"When you start riding dick? Get the fuck off of her nuts. She bleeds just like you and me.

"You's a disrespectful green-eyed bitch. I serve dick, bitch. I don't ride it. You need to think about this. If Ju wants to kill him, then let her. The only person that could handle Boo is dead. You know I ain't never scared, but think about that."

I needed a blunt. That conversation took all of my energy. I was looking around the room trying to spot a cloud of weed smoke. Every time I looked to my left, I caught this lil nigga mugging me. Come to think about it, the whole time Re and I were talking, that lil nigga was hanging around. Jaw came to tell me that he had some LOUD.

"Just go over there and tell my lil brother, Outlaw, to give you a sack."

I almost died when he pointed to the same lil nigga that was ease dropping on Re's and mine conversation. I knew then that it was about to be a problem.

"Man ... fuck!"

My ringing phone only added to my frustration. It was Boo.

"Yo what's up, Boo?"

"LIL MAN IN YO CRIB."

"In my crib?"

"Just get there. He's not alone." I went and grabbed Re and told her what Boo had said.

"Let's go E. Call Young."

Slowly but surely everything was starting to fall apart.

I was impressed at how LJ's spot was running. Every three to five minutes the doorbell was ringing. I might have to head over there and set up shop.

I was trying to take him down. After I told that girl who called and that she was being replaced she hadn't called back. Good! Tonight I was going to try and sink my teeth into his chocolate bar. He was being real attentive to my needs and me tonight. Every few minutes he was checking on me asking if I needed anything. Yep, I was going to make him mine. Who knows?

I could probably get him to take out Lil Man and Jaw. I was just about to ask him to come to the bathroom with me when my sister's ex walked through the door.

"Aw, shit!"

If she saw me, all hell was gonna break loose. She knew that I knew that she was trying to kill my sister. But what blew me outta the water was that LJ walked over to her and greeted her as if they were good friends. I guess my discomfort was written all over my face because LJ's brother, Money Man, said something.

"You good?"

"Yeah, I'm straight. Why?"

"I just saw your whole demeanor change up."

He turned and looked in the direction that E and LJ were in.

"You know that bitch?"

"No."

I had to lie. I didn't want this lil nigga to bust me out.

"Outlaw?"

I watched the younger brother come to where Money Man was standing.

"Aye, go be nosey. I wanna know what that freckle-faced bitch is talking about."

And just like that, Outlaw was gone. I prayed that E didn't tell LJ anything about me. Aw, fuck! In walked that little green-eyed bitch. Fuck! Why were those two bitches looking at me? I knew that she was the killer of the clique. JoJo told me all about that one. I felt so uncomfortable. I got up and headed to the back of the house. I needed to put some distance in between us. Twenty minutes later, Jaw found me.

"What up, ma? I see you done made yourself comfortable."

I was in the bedroom watching T.V.

"Yeah, it got kind noisy out there. I hope you don't mind."

"Na, you good. It looks like ain't shits gon' happen. You ready to go?"

"Only if I'm leaving with you."

He smiled and shook his head.

"We'll see. Come on, let's go.

I was so glad that we were leaving. Just as we were getting ready to leave, I saw E and that other one run up outta there as if they were in a hurry. Bye! I didn't wanna walk past them anyway. His brothers met us at the door. LJ said his goodbyes, and then Money Man turned to me.

"It was nice meeting you."

I liked him. He was quite the little charmer.

"Nice meeting you too, baby."

I turned to tell Outlaw goodbye, but the shitty look he gave me took me by surprise. LJ even caught the look.

"Lil bruh, you cool?"

Outlaw looked dead at me when he spoke.

"Yeah bruh. I'm great. I need to holla at you after you drop shorty off. It's important."

I wonder what the fuck he heard them talking about.

SEVENTEEN

Chapter

Detective Malone

"I'm trying my best to be patient with you. I am not going to keep asking you where that money is. *WHACK* Did you think that I wasn't going to find out? *WHACK* Speak, damn it."

"Fuck you bastard. You better kill me."

I had to laugh at that bitch's boldness. No matter what, cops are supposed to stick together. I took the little bitch in because she was a great asset to my team. But what do I get in return? Betrayal! How dare she open up an investigation on me? I'm the fucking boss. I always cover my ass. I had been having her followed since House was murdered. She was a really a good detective. She found out a lot of shit about me. Smart bitch. I'll die before I let her expose me. My pension was on the line so I had to act fast. I told her to come on a call with me. T tried to pick her brain but that didn't work, so I did what I felt was best. I kidnapped her ass.

"Now you're going to tell me where that money is, you little traitor. You're sleeping with the enemies. Your badge and career are all gone over some little street cunt? Oh, so you're not going to talk? You'll stay right in this basement tied to that chair until you tell me all that I want to know."

I really needed to get in touch with Derrick.

"I'll be back, sugar pants. Don't go nowhere now, ya hear me?"

I was getting too old for this shit. Derrick better have had something good for me because I was fed up with that little weirdo as well.

"Yo? What the hell do you want, Malone?"

"What the hell do I want? Didn't I tell you ... never mind. What did you find in the apartment?"

"Nothing that benefits you. Wasn't no money up in there. I did find some clothes and jewelry."

"I can't do shit with that. Hit the next house on the list. Jay ... Joe."

"Um, Jaw."

"Whatever, just do it. Don't forget we got a new court date. It's the 8th of January."

"All right. I'll be there. Let me call you when I'm ready."

Greed is going to be the death of me, but I don't give a shit. I want that money!

Young Meech

By the time I made it to E's crib, there was nobody there.

"Damn E, they tore this bitch up." She was heated.

"I wanna know what the fuck that nigga was looking for."

"Anything missing?"

"Young, I don't know. What the fuck were Boo and Heidi doing here?"

"Your guess is as good as mine. Something is going on."

I said my goodbyes and bent a couple of corners before I

headed to the crib. Being cooped up in the house playing caregiver was starting to get to me. I needed to find Lil Man so that I could get on with my life. It was a little after 6:00 a.m. when I finally made it in. When I walked in, my houseguest was standing at the window with a gun in her hand.

"Damn, Joe, who you 'bout to shoot?"

"I thought I heard something. Where have you been?"

"I was on my way to Jaw's trap spot when E called me, and told me to meet him at his crib because Lil Man was there."

"In his crib? How did he know that?"

"I guess Boo called him and told him after the shootout."

"SHOOTOUT?"

"Damn, don't yell, but yeah a shootout."

"No luck on finding Lit Man, huh?"

"Not yet. You wanna go find that detective? Ju's court date is in two weeks."

"Yeah, I think I'm ready to show up and drop a few bodies."

Money Man

After Outlaw told me everything that had been said, I was shocked. Big Bruh didn't even know that he was sleeping with the enemy. I needed to seriously holler at him.

"Outlaw, hand me my phone."

I called my brother but he didn't answer the phone. Two seconds later, he called back.

"Money Man, what up, bruh?"

"I need to holla at you AS SOON AS POSSIBLE!"

"You good?"

"Yeah I am, but you're not."

"What you mean?"

"Come holla at me. Bring me some weed, and not that regular shit you brought me last time."

"Nigga that was only that one time. I'm on the way."

I really hoped that Outlaw heard wrong, because if he didn't we were going to kill that pretty green-eyed bitch and her freckle-faced friend. They said that my brother, Jaw, was going to die. They really had life fucked up. Ten minutes later, Jaw came walking in to the trap with a big ass Kool-Aid smile on his face.

"What you so happy about?"

He sat down and started breaking down the sack of weed.

"What's on yo mind, bruh?"

"Shit, murder ... if what Outlaw said was true."

"Let me know something."

"I don't know where to begin. How well do you know ole girl you was with?"

"I just met her, but she is cool people. Why?"

"When that lil dyke bitch came in last night I saw her eyes get big as fuck. I asked her what was wrong, and she told me it was nothing, but she never took her eyes off of y'all. I was curious, so I asked Outlaw to do some detective work and eavesdrop on y'all's conversation. When you walked off, that cute light-skinned chick walked up. Ain't that Poohman's chick?"

"Yeah. Her name is ReRe. That lil bitch is a killer."

"Oh I heard. Guess who's next on her hit list?"

"Who?"

"You!"

"ME? What the fuck I do?"

"Apparently you played her best friend with the girl you was with last night."

"Bruh, I ain't done shit with ole girl."

"Well she answered your phone last week or something."

He dropped his head and shook it back and forth.

"Damn bruh. Ju told me that some bitch answered my phone and told her that she was being replaced. I didn't believe her. But why though?"

"I don't know, but that ain't even the bad part."

"It can't get no worse than that. I fucked up, but I love my girl. I almost went there."

"Almost?"

"Yeah, something was telling me not to fuck her. I let her suck my dick."

I cracked open the Remy and laughed.

"Naw, for real, bruh? Who is Big Moe?"

"Some nigga that Ju and her crew robbed."

"Did he and his cousins die by the hands of one of them?"

"Yeah, why?"

"That bitch you was with last night is Big Moe's cousin."

"WHAT?"

"That bitch ReRe said she was going to definitely kill her. That dyke bitch E told her not to touch you. She told ReRe if Ju wanted to kill you, then that's her job. Not theirs."

I could tell by the look on Jaw's face that he was not expecting that. Then I saw a look that I knew all too well. My brother was about to snap.

"Lil Bruh, thanks for that. I'ma let Re get that bitch. I'm 'bout to call Poohman and let him know to watch his girl. Damn Joe that bitch almost had me."

I was glad I had that talk with my brother. Pussy can cloud a nigga's judgment. Man, we was really about to bring the New Year in with a bang!

Boo

Heidi and I were on the hunt for Ashley. We were on our way to her crib when my phone rang.

"Hello?"

"You have a collect call from Ja'ziya. Press 5 to accept." *beep*

"Hey Ju, how you holding up?"

"I'm not. When is my auntie's funeral?"

"Um, we already had it."

I hated to lie, but I was not about to tell her that I think she was still alive.

"Damn, I couldn't get no fucking obituary?"

I looked at the phone for a second. Did that lil girl just come for me?

"Whoa lil girl. I know you are upset, but you better watch your mouth."

"My bad, Boo. My anger isn't even at you. It's towards Jaw."

"Well, what did he do, baby?"

"Ask him. I'm 'bout to go. I love you. Aw, my trial starts in a few days. On the 8th to be exact."

"I'll be there." *click*

Damn she hung up on me. Heidi's nosey ass was staring me dead in my face.

"What?"

"Don't what me! What did she say?"

"She told me to ask your son."

"Aw never mind. I'm not getting in that shit."

"That shit can wait. Turn right here, and it's the third house from the corner."

As soon as we pulled up, I felt uneasy. I saw Ashley's car

parked in her parking spot. Heidi looked at me and pointed her finger in my face.

"I don't wanna shoot nobody today."

I rolled my eyes and smacked my lips.

"You don't shoot hoe, you fight."

"Well, I don't feel like knocking nobody out today. My hand still hurts."

"You wouldn't be able to fight no way with that damn snow suit on."

"This not no damn snow suit. It's a weather-resistant pullover."

"I hope yo ass is gon' be able to run."

"If I'm running for my life, then I'ma out run you."

When we got to the front door, I could tell that she hadn't been there. The mail was piled up in the mailbox.

"Excuse me, hello? Hi, I'm Ms. Miller and I'm her neighbor. Are you looking for Ashley?"

Heidi jumped in.

"Why are you asking us if we are looking for her?"

"Because why else would you be here?"

"How about you take your nosey ass back in your house and lock the door."

"Excuse me? I was just..."

"You was just about to take yo ugly ass back in yo house before I hit you in the head with a snow ball, bitch!"

I fell out on the stairs. I was laughing so hard that my nose started running. The neighbor practically ran back into her house and snatched her drapes closed.

"Heidi, I need you to hip check the door."

She walked up to the door and grabbed the knob. She was about to give it a bump when it came open.

"Boo, it was unlocked," she said

"I see."

I didn't waste no time pulling my gun out. Her place was wrecked!

"Boo, somebody took her. Either that or she a nasty bitch for keeping her crib like this."

We went through her crib from top to bottom. We found information in her bedroom that led to her boss. She had all types of notes on him.

"Heidi, check the night stand. We need to find an address."

I went to the closet and went through all of her pockets.

"YUCK, BOO! I touched it. I touched it. Gross."

I ran outta the closet to see what the fuck she was yelling about.

"Bitch, why are you screaming like that? You know we aren't 'pose to be in here. You tryin' go to jail?"

"Look!"

"Damn, that motha fucker huge."

Heidi found a big ass dildo. I just shook my head. I don't even want to know who was taking all of that.

"Heidi, put that shit down and go wash your hands."

"I mean, Boo, it's huge," she said

"Girl, go."

I looked in the nightstand and saw an address scribbled on a napkin.

"Heidi, come on. I think I found an address."

"Good, let's get the hell outta here. We 'bout to hit the address up now?"

"We need to suit up first. I think we are gon' need some help. Don't you wanna call Money Man?"

"Might as well call Outlaw, too."

"I hope that girl ain't dead."

"Me too, Heidi. Me too!"

EIGHTEEN

Chapter

ReRe

I have been on a little stake out. I'm watching Jaw's ass like a hawk. After we left the trap, I've literally been in that nigga's backyard. I prayed that he was bold enough to bring that bitch or any bitch to my bestie's crib. Tonight was no different. I told Poohman that I had a few moves to make. He kissed me and I was on my way. I stopped at the liquor store and bought me a pint of Grey Goose. After that, I posted up behind the building that Jaw shared with Ju. I turned on my radio and Meek Mill's *Who You Around* was playing. I closed my eyes and took a drink. I still hadn't shed one tear for Tiki. Not one. Tonight I was sad. My heart hurt. A part of me was truly gone. Before I knew it, I was wiping tears from my eyes.

"Damn, Tiki, I miss you so much girl."

It was as if I heard her tell me that she missed me as well. The floodgates opened and I broke down.

"Somebody who you're around wants to clip your wings and shoot ya down, but it's okay to keep enemies close, as long as you know, just make sure you know who you're around."

The one and only time I was dumb enough to show weakness was the wrong time. I wasn't the only one watching Jaw's crib that night.

Lil Man

"Man, Joe, come on. You ain't gon' need all that."

I was trying to get to Jaw's crib before he made it home. My cousins were taking forever.

Baby Dro was sporting this big ass black eye. Every time I looked at him, I laughed. He knew it, too.

"What the fuck do you keep looking at?"

"Nigga, yo eye!"

"How 'bout I make yo eye look like mine."

"You and what army, pussy?"

The nigga actually stood up and walked towards me until KeeKee jumped in.

"Y'all cool that shit out. We got shit to do tonight. Settle it later."

He walked off and I had to just ask him.

"Baby Dro, how you gon' get mad at me? That lady knocked yo ass out, not me."

He turned and looked at me. He was mad as hell.

"You keep playing with me boy, and I'ma do something to you."

I threw my hands up in the air.

"Nigga, I got a hit out on me. You think I'm worried about you?"

After we got our shit together, we headed out. We brought out the big guns today. I was ready.

"Park around the back. I don't wanna have another shootout."

I needed to at least stay alive long enough to kill them other two bitches as well as Young. My cousin, BayBay, tapped my shoulders, taking me away from my thoughts.

"Whud up, Bay?"

He pointed to a dark green two-door Cutlass with a girl in it crying her eyes out. I took a closer look, and when I noticed whom that girl was, my dick became as hard as hell.

"Oh shit, BayBay, that's one of them hoes I'm looking for."

I must admit I was a little bit on the shocked side because ReRe was the one in the clique that would kill you and your whole family. Now she's sitting in front of me crying like a weak ass bitch. Baby Dro felt as if he had something to prove since that old lady knocked his ass out. He was the first one to try and run up.

"Wait, Baby Dro!"

ReRe

I released so many tears that I felt dehydrated. I just blamed it on the Goose.

"Damn, Re, get yourself together."

I leaned over to reach in the glove compartment to grab some tissues when I thought I saw somebody creeping up to my car. I grabbed my Glock .40 and cocked it. Whoever that nigga was trying to run up on me was about to die a quick death. I hit the down button on my window and heard somebody scream.

"Wait, Baby Dro."

Now he was running full speed towards me.

"Oh yeah, nigga?" *BOC, BOC, BOC, BOC*

"BABY DRO!"

Each one of my bullets hit their mark. That nigga crumbled at the front of my car. I saw three more niggas running through the darkness towards my car so I dropped my car in gear and accelerated. *Bump Bump* I ran over the nigga that I shot and then sped towards the other three dudes. At the last second, they all jumped out of the way. The face I saw before I made my getaway pissed me off even more because I wish I coulda shot him instead.

"Lil Man?" heard him screaming.

"I'MA KILL YOU, BITCH!"

I grabbed my phone and called Jaw.

"Yo what up, Re?"

"Lil man and some niggas was just outside yo crib. I hit one of em. You need to get there."

"WHAT?"

"Nigga you heard me. Get there!"

I hung up and called Poohman. That nigga was stalking now? He had to go.

Lil Man

"WHAT THE FUCK JUST HAPPENED?"

I told that hotheaded ass nigga to wait. Now the nigga was dead, surprisingly, his brothers didn't chew an ounce of emotion. That shit scared me. Nothing scares me, but that did!

"Come on, BayBay; help me carry him to the front of the building."

After carrying him to the front, KeeKee called the police.

I just came outside, and there was a dead body lying on the ground. *Click*

He looked at me, and for the first time ever I saw KeeKee cry.

"Take me to that nigga's trap now!"

NINETEEN

Chapter

Jaw

After Money Man told me what Outlaw heard Dirty and ReRe talking about, I felt stupid. Funky bitch! That's what the fuck I get for thinking with my dick. I swear I'm gonna murder that bitch. First thing I was going to do was find out who her connect was; then I was going to rob her dumb ass. When all was said and done, I was dropping her ass off in Lake Michigan. *ring ring* I didn't expect to see ReRe's number pop up on my screen. What the fuck did she want? I mean, just a few days earlier she was talking about killing me, and now she's calling me?

"Yo, what up, ReRe?"

"Lil Man and some niggas was just outside yo crib. I hit one of them. You need to get there."

"WHAT?"

"You heard me, get there!"

Man, what the hell is really going on? Should I even trust that shit? Her ass was probably waiting on me. How the fuck did she even know that Lil Man was outside of my crib? I'm 'bout to get to the bottom of this shit. I grabbed my phone and called the one person that I knew could handle her.

"What up, Jaw. Where you at, boy? I'm at your crib, and out

back, there's a trail of blood. Those peoples are everywhere."

Damn, she wasn't lying.

"I just got a call from yo girl telling me that Lil Man was outside of my crib with some niggas, and she hit one of them."

"That's what she told me."

"You say there's a blood trail in the back?"

"Yep."

"ReRe said that she hit one of 'em. What the fuck was she doing posted up in the alley behind my crib, bruh?"

"Man, just get here. I'm out here. I want them niggas to come back.

"I'm on my way."

Man, I didn't know what to think. ReRe posted up outside my crib. Lil Man and some niggas creeping around my spot. What else could go wrong?

Money Man

I wonder why the hell Jaw ran up outta here like that. Something was going on, so I came up over here. This spot was a gold mine. Whatever you wanted, we had. We didn't have to worry about the police because big bruh had 'em in his pockets. Now as far as them jack boys went, I wanted one of them to run up in here. I was definitely going to make an example out of one of them. I decided to chill and drink something. Tonight was a little on the slow side. I wasn't tripping though because New Year's was gonna be jumping.

"Hey Boo? Go run to the store and get us something to drink."

"Us, huh?"

"Please."

"Please, my ass."

"Oh I plan to."

"Whatever. Where my gun at?"

"You ain't gon' need it. I'll have Outlaw or Skee roll with you."

"No, I want my gun, and you can tell Skee to come on. Outlaw's ass been smoking all day. He on some tweekin' shit."

I handed her the money and told her to hurry up and come back. She turned around and stuck her tongue out at me. I just smiled. My girl was a rider.

Lil Man

We sat patiently down the street from the trap spot. Fuck all that creeping and sneaking. Every time we took that approach, you saw what happened. My cousins were very quiet and that made me uncomfortable. KeeKee cocked his pistol and opened the door. BayBay and I quickly followed suit. While we were walking up the street, we saw a girl and some dude leaving out.

"KeeKee, what's the plan?"

"Everyone dies!'

Outlaw

I'm an action junky. I don't want to do shit but make money and shoot shit up. I have been trying to get down with my big brother, Jaw, since forever. I told him that I was the only enforcer that he needed. I wasn't playing Duck Hunt for all those years for nothing. I 'm young as hell, but I found something that I was good at. Shooting! Tonight was the night that I stayed in the back room playing video games. It was slow, and I didn't want to play escort walking Money Man's girl to the store all damn day. I heard the door open so I jumped up to see what was going on. I saw Spooky and Skee leaving. I scanned the streets looking for anything to be out of order. This was the time of night that niggas roamed the streets looking for something to rob.

My eyes zoomed in on a White Tahoe that was parked a few cars back. I could see that there were three niggas in the truck. They appeared to be watching something. Since Spooky and Skee just walked out, I assumed that it was them that they were watching. The doors to the truck popped open and they rushed up to the porch.

"I know them niggas ain't about to do what I think."

All of a sudden, I saw one of them niggas run towards Spooky and Skee.

"AW SHIT, MONEY MAN. JACK BOYS!"

Money Man

After my girl and Skee left, I sat back on the couch and lit a blunt. Even though it was slow, today's take was on point. I needed to ask Jaw for some extra dough. I was trying to hit the studio. Not even two minutes after I sat down, I heard Outlaw scream.

"AW SHIT, MONEY MAN. JACK BOYS!"

I jumped straight up and grabbed the AR-15 from up under the couch. Outlaw came flying outta the back room with the Tec-9.

"Come on, bruh. They rushing Spooky and Skee."

I opened the door just in time to see my homie's head explode like a melon.

"Fuck, Skee!"

I was frantically searching for my girl. I couldn't find her After Skee's body dropped, those three niggas came running towards us. I stepped back in the house and pulled the trigger. *TAT, TAT, TAT, TAT, TAT* Bullets were flying everywhere. I heard Outlaw scream.

"Y'all got us fucked up."

One nigga screamed, "Aw shit, I'm hit."

The dude that I hit ran back out of the door.

"Outlaw, don't let that nigga get away."

The other two guys started backing up. I guess they ran out of bullets.

My gun jammed, so I ran in the kitchen to grab my Glock. Running back to the door, I heard Outlaw yell.

"Spooky, watch out!" *BOC, BOC, BOC*

My heart dropped to the pit of my stomach. I ran out the front door expecting the worse. My girl was standing over the nigga that I had shot with her gun pointed at his head. She looked up at me and her eyes were glazed over as if she had checked out. Outlaw ran to grab Spooky.

"Come on sis, we gotta go before the police come."

She looked at me and shook her head. Damn, my shorty just domed that nigga. We grabbed what we needed and got the fuck out of dodge. Jaw was going to kill us!

Lil Man

We fled the scene another man short. BayBay didn't make it. I was scared to even say shit to KeeKee. He was driving like a bat outta hell.

"Man, Joe, slow this motha fucka down before we get pulled

over. Nigga, don't forget we got guns in here."

He slowed and looked at me.

"Nigga, because of your shit, I just lost both of my brothers. You should have let me know what we was walking into."

I didn't even respond. I told those niggas that it could get bloody. If I said something, it was going to be him or me. Hell, we both might die if he didn't slow this truck down.

"Lil Man?"

"Yeah, cuz."

"I'ma call a few of my hit squad niggas. You gon' show me where every last one of them motha fuckers stay."

"I got you, cuz. Let's get those niggas."

TWENTY

Chapter

JoJo

I had been feeding E all type of info on Lil Man. I wished she would hurry and kill his ass. I was sick and tired of looking at him. The more he touched me, the deader I wanted him. I don't even think deader is a word, but that's how I feel. My damn sister has been around here on cloud nine. She told me that she was seeing some dude name LJ. Bitch has been neglecting her sisterly duties. Like now, I was hungry, had a slight case of morning sickness, and my feet was hurting. Do you think that bitch offered to help me out? I told her I was hungry.

"You better get yo lazy ass up and cook yo self. I got a date."

"Let me guess, LJ?"

She smiled and flung her hair.

"Don't hate."

"Girl, hate on what? You better get yo life together. Where you going tonight?"

"We are supposed to be going to the House of Blues."

"Well, have fun."

I got up and went to the window because I heard a car pulling up.

"Who is out there with a baby blue Charger?"

She came flying to the window.

"Aw, that's my boo, LJ."

I had to squint my eyes to get a better view. When I saw who LJ really was, I almost threw up. I started cracking up.

"What the hell is so funny?"

I walked off.

"You'll find out, dummy!"

 Boo

Finding out about the attempt on Re's life pissed me off. I was livid. Lil Man was walking a thin line between life and death. I had to call Jaw.

"Yo, what up, auntie?"

"I need you to find Lil Man, like yesterday."

"I already know. That nigga tried to hit my crib and the spot. Money Man and Outlaw shot it out with him and two other niggas. I know where he lays his head. I just gotta catch him slipping."

"What you mean? Kinda like he has been catching y'all? I heard about what he tried to do to Re."

"But the crazy part about that was why the fuck she was even posted up in the back of my crib? I think she's watching me."

"Why would she be watching you?"

He became real quiet.

"Talk nigga!"

"Man, auntie, I fucked up and let this bitch get too close to me. She answered my phone one day when I left her in my car. She told Ju that she was replacing her. So, I'm sure Ju told Re, and she has probably been watching me ever since."

I been knowing this lil boy since he was a sperm cell in his daddy's balls. He wasn't telling me everything.

"And what else, Jaw? Don't tell me half. Tell me all."

"Damn, auntie. Okay, look ... the lil bitch just so happens to be Big Moe's cousin. Outlaw heard Dirty and ReRe talking about it the other night."

"So you had no idea?"

"I ain't never met that hoe before. Remember the lil hoe Dirty was fucking with?"

"JoJo?"

"Yeah, well that's her sister."

I just shook my head.

"See, you lil dumb ass lil boy. Your dick was almost the death of you. I see why ReRe was watching you. She was waiting to catch you with that girl."

I just laughed because that damn ReRe was certified.

"Boy, you better fix this before I fix you. Get off of my line, dumb ass."

I hung up on that damn fool. Damn, I really needed Pete right now. He was my eyes and ears to the streets. They never found his killer. I had my own idea on who killed him but now he's dead, too. I needed to get up with Heidi so we could do a drive by. I knew what Malone's car looked like. I just needed to check the address that we found at Ashley's.

"What the hell you want? Today I'm staying in the house with my grandbabies. Do you ever quit?"

"For real, Heidi? You are staying in the house with them bad ass kids to do what?"

"I'm baking cookies, bitch."

I started laughing my ass off.

"You don't even know how to bake."

"And? They don't know that. What do you want?"

"I need you to ride by this house with me. I think that it is the detective's crib."

"Aw hell naw. Every time we go looking for trouble, Boo, we find it and then some. Ain't you tired of getting shot at? I know I am."

"It's not even like that today. We're just gonna ride by and peep out the scene.

"You are a liar and a fat mouth. What are we possibly looking for?"

"I think he took Ashley."

"So call the police."

"He is the police."

"Then call the other police. The police bigger than him. Leave that shit for them. I'm not trying to die before the New Year."

"Come on scaredy cat. That girl could be in trouble. Remember she did save our lives."

I had to throw it on thick and make her feel bad.

"That was low, Boo. You didn't have to throw that shit in my face. You better pray that she ain't up in there. We gon' fuck around and need some help our damn selves."

"I'll be there in 20 minutes."

"Whatever!"

Just to make the shit even better for Heidi, I went to Jaw's crib and got Outlaw and Money Man.

"Bring y'all asses on."

I needed more fire power. Better to be safe than sorry. After I scooped up Heidi, we got to the address in no time.

"Damn, Boo, these houses are huge."

I thought so, too.

"Yeah they are. You think they are big enough to hide a body?"

Heidi gave me the 'be quiet' look.

"It's kids in the car."

That shit just tickled me.

"Kids, my ass. Don't ignore the fact that they just had a shootout in Englewood the other day."

Heidi's eyes popped out of her head.

"They did, huh?"

She took off her belt and was about to start swinging.

"Uh, ummm ... bitch, don't you hit my nephews. They were protecting the spot, and they didn't even start it."

She thought about it for a minute.

"Fuck all that. I'm beating y'all asses later."

Young Meech

Today my mentor and I were going to go pay that detective dude a visit. He needed to be dead before Ju's trial started. Without him, there was no case. Lil Man wasn't going to make it either. I walked back in the bedroom to see if she was ready. I just stood there in awe. I mean, damn, she was a sight to look at. She had put on a few pounds since the accident. Her skin had cleared up tremendously. Only a few red marks still covered her face. She wore her hair short and spiky. I liked it. She looked brand new.

"Lil boy, quit staring at me like that before I kick yo ass. Your eyes tell me exactly what you're thinking."

I was busted. If I were like three years older, I would have shot my shot. I felt my cheeks burning and shit.

"My bad, you just look good. How do you feel?"

"Desperate."

"Huh?"

121

"We only got one shot to get this done. If we miss, we'll never get the chance again. He's going to do everything in his power to bury my niece. So get your mind outta the gutter and let's go get that motha fucka!"

I was more than ready. The sooner we got Malone, the sooner I could get Lil Man.

"You driving, lady."

We hit the expressway, and the only sound that could be heard was the outside wind whipping the car around. Today was a cold day, and I wasn't talking about the weather. It was cold because I had no remorse about the lives that were about to be taken. I learned a lot nursing my mentor back to health. She taught me that love is forbidden in these streets.

In this game, love will get me killed. Losing Tyesha was my lesson learned. I was supposed to protect her and I failed. The streets don't love anybody. I can kill now and not think twice about it. That innocent boy that I once was is gone. Dead! Today, I stand-alone. The beast in me is dying to be released. I think it's time to let him out.

"Earth to Young. Boy, where the hell you just go?"

"Man, you don't even wanna know. Whud up though?"

"We're here!"

We had to be in the suburbs. These houses were massive.

"Where does he stay?"

She pointed behind us.

"Four houses that way. We are gon' creep through a back window or something."

I grabbed my Desert Eagle from under the seat and checked the chamber.

"I'm ready, ma."

She checked her weapon and grabbed the door handle. She

122

stopped and turned back around to look at me.

"What?"

"Don't ever call me ma again, lil boy."

Detective Malone

I was so frustrated. I had been torturing that bitch for the last two weeks, and she still wouldn't break. I was tired of her ass whining and crying.

I was even nice enough to feed her, and what was the thanks I got? Nothing!

"I'm going to give you one last chance to tell me what I wanna know."

I pulled the tape off of her mouth so that she could speak.

"You're going to kill me anyway. *Patoo*

She spit in my face.

"Fuck you!"

I punched her so hard in her throat that she threw up all over the floor. I jumped back not wanting to get any of that shit on me. It was time for me to call the cleanup crew. I was tired of fucking around with her ass.

"Have it your way. I'll see you in hell."

I needed to hurry up and get rid of that bitch. My basement was a wreck. There was piss and shit all over the place. You would have thought that I had a damn puppy. I picked up the phone to make a very important call.

"Hey Jimmie, I need a favor. I had a party and made a huge mess. Can you send your boys to come clean?"

I looked at my watch. Shit! I needed to run to the store to play the lottery. The pot was up to $473 million. If I won that, I was moving to a whole other country. I took one last look at Dixon and shook my head.

"What a waste."

"I think that's the house right there, Heidi."

"How you know?"

"Because it's the address we found at Ashley's."

"Look, Boo. There that fat ass bastard goes right over there."

He was walking out of the house headed for his black Crown Vic parked at the curb.

"Okay, Heidi, let Money Man and Outlaw walk up and down the street keeping watch. Me and you are going to go through a window or something."

Before she could respond, Outlaw's lil badass wanted to put his two cents in, "Man, auntie, that plan is whack as hell."

I had to look him up and down, you know sizing his lil ass up. I was about to get Heidi's belt and beat his ass myself.

"Boy, who the hell you talking to? I didn't ask you shit."

"Auntie, think about it. Look around. We don't even look like we belong over here."

Damn, he had a point. I wasn't about to let his ass know it though.

"Let me and Money Man break in."

He paused to look at his momma.

"We kinda sorta know how to get in people's houses."

Heidi popped his ass in the forehead.

"That's for everything that I don't know about."

Young Meech

"I'm following your lead."

I watched her move. She moved like a cat, low to the ground and quick. I had a hard time keeping up with her. I was the one in shape, or so I thought. When she finally stopped, we were in the back of that detective's house.

"So Tomb Raider, what's the plan?"

She put her finger to my mouth and shushed me.

"Do you hear that?"

I got closer to the window so that I could listen. I thought I heard somebody crying, but I wasn't sure.

"I'm about to climb through the window. When I check things out, you can come behind me."

She motioned for me to go ahead. I tried the window and was happy as shit that it was unlocked. I climbed in, checked around, and then ran back to the window to help her inside. We both instantly pulled out our guns when we heard a female scream.

"Meech, what the fuck?"

"It's coming from that back room."

As we walked towards the screaming, the smell of piss and shit burned the hair out of my nose. I had to swallow the vomit that danced in the back of my throat. There was a padlock on the door.

"Fuck! If I shoot that lock, it's gonna be loud as hell."

She stepped back and with one swift kick. *BOOM* Damn. The door went flying off of the hinges. I flipped the light on in the room; and what little emotion that I had left, almost made me break down. "Damn, Ash."

"Meech, untie her and pick her up."

She was bound and gagged. The room was full of shit and piss. Her once beautiful skin was now covered in scratches and sores. When she realized that it was me, she completely broke down. We were so focused on rescuing her that we didn't pay attention to the fact that we were no longer alone.

Money Man

After finally convincing my momma and Boo that Outlaw and I should go in first, it was now time to get shit cracking.

"Come on Outlaw. We are gon' hit the back of the house and find a window. You know how we do."

"How you know that there's going to be a window that's unlocked?"

"I don't know. We in the white folks' neighborhood. They don't lock they windows boy."

We found an open window. Even better.

"Outlaw, go allow Boo and momma in."

When we made it in, I immediately smelled a strong ass odor. Outlaw took off running to let them in, while I investigated where the smell was coming from. I pulled out my lil two-shot Dillinger and made my way to the end of the basement. The closer I got, the worse the smell became.

"Damn, it stinks."

I should have waited on Outlaw to come back. Not even two seconds after I went to peep out the scenery I had a hand over my mouth and a gun pointed at my head.

"Don't scream."

Damn, I was in trouble. I don't know if it was the strong stench of piss and shit that had me hallucinating, but the lady that

126

appeared before me looked just like Lil Mama. You only see the dead when you're about to join 'em.

"Heidi, when we get in here be on point, because anything can happen."

She had the nerve to roll her eyes at me.

"Why you doing all that?"

"Bitch, I'm always on point. Don't try me like that."

"Well my bad. Oh, look. Come on, Outlaw is at the door."

We walked up to the house as if we belonged there. Thank God that I didn't see any nosey ass neighbors.

"Outlaw? Where is Money Man?"

"I left him in the basement."

"What the fuck is that smell?"

Heidi was about to throw up all over the floor until I pushed her ass towards the laundry sink.

"Bitch, don't throw up on this floor. Your DNA will be all over the place."

I was kinda waiting for Money Man to jump out and scare us. He was known for that shit. One night I was so drunk he jumped out of the bushes with a Michael Myers mask on. I pissed all the way down my leg. I hoped that he wasn't in the mood to play because I might accidently shoot his ass.

"Money Man, bring yo ass out."

I was expecting my nephew to come out. When she appeared before me, it was almost too much for me to bear.

Damn sis, yo nosey ass is always in the middle of something."

"Lil Mama?"

ReRe

E ver since Lil Man tried to shoot me, I've been laying low. I was gonna catch his ass. It was only a matter of time. Poohman and I had been at odds for the last few days. I don't know why, but the silent treatment was starting to irk the fuck outta me.

"Poohman. What's your problem?"

"I should be asking you the same question. Why were you even parked in the back of Jaw's crib that night Lil Man tried to get at you?"

Now should I lie? See this was where things got tricky. Jaw is his best friend, and I'm sure that he was going to defend him, right, wrong, or indifferent.

"You don't have to think about no answer."

Ohhh, he's mad. Fuck it. Wasn't no need to lie.

"I was watching his crib to see if he was going to bring that bitch I saw him with there."

I guess he wasn't expecting that answer.

"Re, that ain't none of your business."

Wrong answer!

"Oh, but it is. That nigga ain't about to play my girl while she's down and out."

"I understand your concern, but..."

"'But,' my ass. That nigga is in violation, and if you are condoning his actions I might start looking at you in a different way."

"That man is grown, Re."

"He's also stupid. Do you know that the bitch that he is spending so much time with is Big Moe's cousin?"

He had a puzzled look on his face.

"Yeah, I cracked yo damn face huh? Say something."

"I knew it was something about that girl that I didn't like."

"And you just let your friend hang with her anyway? Some friend you are."

"He's grown."

"Well, I'm letting you know now that I'm going to kill that bitch."

"Don't get in that shit."

"Oh I'm in, and you are, too. You better be lucky I'm not tryin' to kill your friend. I'll leave that up to JuJu."

"I wonder, does he know?"

"It don't matter. That bitch will be a distant memory by the new year."

"Damn, ma, you cold? I love that shit though."

"Oh yeah? Come show me how much."

JoJo had been all up in her feelings lately. I couldn't care less though. I was trying to win that nigga over so he could do all my dirty work. Lil Man hasn't been here in a few days. Fine by me. I swear that little maniac gives me the creeps. Today, me and my boo had plans. He rented a cabin up in Wisconsin somewhere. I was geeked up. Finally, I was going to be able to put this pussy in his life and lock him down. I took my time getting ready. I even played nice and cooked JoJo something to eat.

"Come eat, lil girl."

She came in the kitchen looking as if she had an attitude. You going out with LJ again?"

"Yup, why? You jealous?"

She started laughing hard as hell. What I said wasn't even funny.

"What's so funny?"

"Aw nothing. Have you called Jaw lately and fed him some more info on Lil Man?"

"To be honest with you, I haven't. Haven't had time. I have got a whole different agenda now. I'm gonna pussy whip LJ. I can make a nigga do whatever I want after that."

"I see."

I didn't like how she was trying to doubt my skills. I was gonna make her young, dumb ass a believer.

"How many phones do LJ have?"

"Two, why?"

"Do you have both numbers?"

"I got the personal line. What's with all the questions?"

"You should know everything there is to know about a man that you are trying to lock down."

"Thanks for that advice. By the way, how are you and your serial killer baby daddy doing?"

"You trying to be funny, but I'm not laughing. Thanks for the food. Have fun!"

That was the reason why I didn't want kids. That baby got her head and her hormones all fucked up.

Jaw

I made plans to get Mia as far away from the city as I could. I planned to really do her dirty after I dicked her down, of course. What? A dick-whipped bitch will tell you everything. I needed to holla at Poohman to see how we were gonna go about reopening the spot.

"What up, Poohman?"

"Man, Joe, where the fuck you at?"

"I've been laying low, what's good?"

"Tell me you ain't know that hoe you been with is Big Moe's cousin?"

Damn, how did he know? I never thought that ReRe would tell him since she was planning on killing ole girl and me.

"I just found that out. I'ma handle her ass though."

"I'll never say this in front of nobody, but you know you are wrong."

"I know I fucked up, but I'ma get my girl back."

"Let me know if you need me."

"I do."

"Anything, bruh."

"Keep yo girl away from me."

"Nigga, yo scary ass."

"Man you know how yo girl is. I'm trying to see another new year."

Jo Jo

I know you might think that I'm wrong for not telling my sister that her precious LJ was, in fact, the Jaw that she was

131

eventually supposed to kill, but she was walking around here feeling herself. Fuck her. She's for self now, and so am I. Derrick hasn't been here in a few days. I didn't know whether to be happy or worried. I was more than worried that his ass was still alive. E told me that she was going to help me get out of town. A part of me believed her, but the street-smart JoJo thought otherwise. I was prepared for the worst. I stayed strapped! *Ring, Ring* Who the hell would be calling me this late? Damn, it was Derrick.

"Hello?"

"Whud up, baby mama?"

I almost threw up when he said that.

"Where have you been?"

I had to at least act as if I cared.

"I been in these streets handling grown folks business. I need you to do something for me."

"What?"

"Sound excited bitch before I come beat yo ass."

I hated this nigga.

"Anything for you, boo. What you need?"

"I need you to call that nigga Dirty and try to get him alone."

What the fuck? Was he serious?

"Uh, um, I ... why would you even put me and your baby in harm's way? You know that bitch wants me dead just as bad as you do."

I thought that maybe the guilt trip role would work. I forgot whom I was talking to. He didn't give a fuck about his own life. How the hell should I expect him to care about mine?

"I'll be there with you. Don't worry, I'll protect you."

I could have sworn I just heard him giggle.

"All right, when are you coming?"

"Soon." *Click!*

He was such a fucking loser. I needed to call E.

Dirty E

"Nigga, you lying! Are you serious? I'm 'bout to slide on you after I take care of some business."

I hung up the phone and kinda just sat there in a zone. Young just told me that Lil Mama wasn't dead. What type of shit was that? He also said that they were at that detective dude's house waiting for him to come home. That's crazy. I needed to get up to the county so I could tell JuJu the good news. I hit ReRe to see if she wanted to go with me.

"Whud up, Freckles?"

She knew I hated when she called me that.

"You so disrespectful. Anyway, guess what?"

"No. Tell me."

"Smart ass. Young just told me that Lil Mama ain't dead."

It was quiet for like 10 seconds. I thought she hung up.

"Re?"

"Yeah, I'm here. I don't know what to say. We need to hit the county and tell JuJu."

"My point exactly."

"But I can't go right now."

"Why not?"

"Because I'm posted outside JoJo's crib waiting for her sister."

I started cracking up. That girl was a fool.

"Bestie, why?"

"Poohman's dumb ass slipped up and told me that Jaw was going up to some cabin in Wisconsin. Well, I'm sure that he's not going by himself. He will if I can catch that bitch first."

"What you gon' do?"

"Do I really have to tell you?"

"Come on, Re, now's not the time. When the time is right, I'll make sure you get your rocks off."

I could tell that she wasn't trying to hear me. I had to butter her up.

"You know I got that bitch JoJo wrapped around my finger. I'll make sure you get her sister I promise. Just not now."

"When then?"

"Soon. Meet me at my crib. We need somebody to come up to the county with us. *Beep* Hold on, my other is line beeping. As a matter of fact, just get here."

I clicked over and to my surprise, it was JoJo.

"What's up girl?"

"Nothin. Um, Lil Man wants me to set you up."

"Oh yeah?"

"Yeah. He's supposed to be coming back over here. Come through. Just bring back up, and E, be careful."

TWENTY-TWO

Chapter

Boo

"**L**il Mama?"

She came out of the shadows and walked up to me. She looked different. She was the same, but she wasn't. She had gained a few pounds. Her once long and curly hair was all gone. She was rocking this short, spiky Mohawk style. It was different for her, but it worked.

"Stop staring at me. I'm good. As a matter of fact, I'm better."

She was so lucky that we were in someone else's home. I would have kicked her ass.

"Why not reach out to me? I'm your sister. And you!"

I turned to look at Meechie. I wanted to curse him out so bad. How could he keep that shit from me? She was my sister. I thought a part of me had died. Heidi stepped up and broke the silence.

"I should kick yo boney ass for making Boo worry like that."

Lil Mama smiled and shook her head.

"Was Boo the only one worried?"

I looked at Heidi and thought I saw a tear.

"Hell yeah, Boo was the only one worried. I don't even like you like that."

We all shared a laugh. I looked around in pure disgust.

"What's going on down here?"

No sooner than I said that, I hear a cough coming from around the corner. I walked to where Lil Mama were standing and looked to my left.

"Oh my god, Ashley!"

Poor thing. She was in bad shape. I ran to her and attempted to grab her. The stench that came from her was too much to bear.

"Money Man? You and Meechie get her out of here."

As if it wasn't already enough tension in the air, Money Man was mugging Meech.

"Why are you looking at him like that?"

"That nigga pulled a gun on me."

"Oh boy, shut the fuck up, and do what the hell I told you to do."

I looked around for something to wrap her up in. Lil Mama helped me wrap her up in a blanket, and we helped Meech get her out of the back window. After that was done, it was time to go.

"Lil Mama, come on. Me, you, Heidi, and Outlaw gon' walk out of the front door like we are one big happy family."

"You all can go. I'm waiting for his fat ass to come back."

Did I just hear her right?

"Why are you waiting?"

"Because he is the only thing standing in the way of my niece's freedom.

I have been watching him for a long ass time. He even paid Lil Man to cut my damn brakes.

"All right, let me round up some of my goons. I'll hit you back."

Damn, that nigga must be getting desperate. I needed to be on shit at all times. Too much has been going on. I couldn't afford to lose another loved one. Speaking of loved ones, I really needed to call Young back.

"Young, what's ...?"

"Man, Joe, they in trouble."

"What's wrong?"

"Boo, Heidi, Lil Mama, and Outlaw are trapped the house. Dude came back."

"WHAT? Man, shoot me the address. I'm on the way."

After he told me the address, I jumped on the expressway.

"Man, E you gotta hurry up. We gotta get up out of here."

I hung up and called Re back.

"What captain saved a hoe?"

"Meet me at this address. Young and 'em are in trouble."

"Aw shit, we got action?"

"Hell yeah. Bring ya gun!"

"But he's a cop. You can't..."

"And you can?"

No this bitch didn't? Okay, she had a point.

"Whoa, Lil Mama, what's the plan?"

I followed her upstairs to the dining room area.

"You should be worried, too, Boo."

"Why?"

She pointed to the table.

"Aw, hell naw!"

It was surveillance photos of me coming out of my house ... and me at the store. Hell, there was even one with me pulling my panties out of my ass.

"What the hell is all this?" Lil Mama laughed.

"He was watching you, too."

That shit didn't sit well with me. I looked through the rest of the pictures and almost peed on myself.

"Ohhh, Lil Mama, look."

He had dates and times to where we would be, and pictures of some of us doing some illegal shit.

"If the courts got a hold of thi..."

My words were cut short when Outlaw came flying down stairs screaming, "That nigga home. We got to move."

Heidi gave him the evil eye.

"What the hell were you doing upstairs?"

Outlaw smiled and said, "Going through his stuff."

Detective Malone

"What do you mean you can't come clean? I paid you good money in advance, and this is what you do? I'll fix your ass." *Click!*

I didn't want to clean all that shit and piss up. I needed to get that shit taken care of though. What I did know was that bitch in my basement was seconds away from the crossroads. Fuck it. I was just gonna have to get my hands dirty. When I pulled onto my block, I immediately noticed something that wasn't right. There was a black truck sitting a few feet from my driveway. Call me paranoid, but I have never seen that truck before. I had to tell myself to get a grip. I mean, it was the holiday season. Family came to visit relatives. That's what it was. One of my neighbor's relatives. I was just tripping. I got out and got ready to walk up to my front door when someone called me.

"Um, excuse me, detective, can I have a word with you please? It will only take a few seconds."

Damn! This has got to be one of the nosiest people that I have ever met.

"Yes, Ms. Winterburg. How can I help you?"

"Um, I could be wrong, but I thought I saw a young lady creeping through your yard. She had on all black. I swear I thought she was like a ninja."

I had to hide my frustration.

"Thank you very much. I'll be on alert."

Could she be telling the truth? I didn't believe that old ass bat. She was always making shit up. Hell, I almost shot the mailman because she said he was trying to break into her house. I thanked her and headed to the front door. When I opened the door, I was hit so hard in my stomach that I almost shit on myself.

"God damn it."

The bitch that hit me was bouncing around as if she was Rocky Balboa in the ring.

"Yeah, you bitch ass nigga. I told you that I was gonna get yo fat ass."

I looked up and saw my suspect's mother. *WHAM!* She hit me again.

"Bitch, I'm gonna..." *WHAM, WHAM*

"Heidi, that's enough. We can't talk to him if you knock his ass out."

I was dizzy and incoherent. Damn, that bitch hit me hard as hell. I knew that I was in trouble. I had to do something.

"Drag him down the stairs," I heard one of them say. If they got me in that basement, I was dead. I was being dragged through my own home. I was about to plead my case until I saw her.

"No, it can't be."

She smiled.

"Oh yes it can. Say goodbye, motha fucker!"

Lil Mama

After everything that I've been through, here I was risking my freedom for the freedom of my niece. Was I wrong? This fat bastard was willing to ruin my niece's life because he wanted some money. I was going to enjoy killing him.

"Drag his ass downstairs."

I was going to tie him up in that same filthy room he kept Ashley in. As I watched Outlaw and Boo drag him down the stairs, I saw a glimpse of something in his hand. Shit!

A GUN!

The first shot grazed Boo's arm.

"Shit, that nigga hit me."

I grabbed Outlaw's hand.

"Let him go."

I almost laughed when Outlaw kicked him square in his ass sending him flying down the stairs face first.

"Let's go now!"

We took off running like bats outta hell. I snatched Outlaw and pulled him towards my car. We jumped in and Meech pulled off. Meech was frantic.

"What the hell happened in there? I was scared as shit. I thought he was going to get y'all."

I closed my eyes and put my head back on the seat.

"We fucked up!"

All I could think about was how my niece might spend the rest of her life in jail because I didn't kill him. I failed her.

TWENTY-THREE

Chapter

Dirty E

"What? Don't come? All right I'll meet y'all there then." Damn, Re gon' be mad. I hit up Re and told her the same thing. Well, there goes my action for the day. Seriously, things were getting out of control. We all needed to lay low, at least until Ju beat her case. I called JoJo to see where her head was.

"Aye, meet me somewhere."

"I can't. *He's* here."

"You good?"

"No. He and his cousin are in the living room lounging around."

I know that I just said that I was gonna chill, but come on, y'all; I couldn't pass up the chance to get that nigga. I called Re back.

"Nigga, what now? Stop getting my hopes up high."

"For real doe, Lil Man over there on Burnham. You wanna go get that nigga?"

"Damn right I do."

"Meet me over there."

I called JoJo back and told her to get the nigga to come outside.

"I don't think he's gonna leave."

"Well you better try, or you might get shot with his ass because we are coming!"

Jaw

I felt like a fool for stepping out on my girl. And to make matters worse, I was frolicking with the enemy. I was going to make shit right tonight. That bitch, Mia, was about to be reunited with her family members. Before I made that trip, I tried my luck and went to see JuJu. I was as nervous as hell. Even though she was behind the glass, I still felt like she could touch me.

"Visit for Campbell."

I walked over to the desk to sign in."

"You can go back there when the other visitor comes out."

"Other visitor?"

She was being messy as I coached her ass on.

"Come on, ma."

I went in my pocket and dropped a 100-dollar bill. I kicked it under the desk and looked at her. She pointed her finger to the name above mine. "Jae'lyn Hill?"

Who the fuck was that? I had to see for myself. I acted as if the C.O. wasn't even there and walked in to the visiting room. What I saw next enraged me. JuJu was all smiles and shit. I stood there for a few minutes trying to assess the situation before me. Dude checked his watch, kissed his two fingers, and placed them on the glass before he hung up the phone. I wanted her to see me more than ever at that moment. As soon as I made my presence known, everything ceased. JuJu actually looked at me and smiled. I ignored her ass and approached the nigga.

"Whud up, homie? Where you know my wife from?"

He stared at me for a second.

"Your wife, huh? Ask her?"

He walked off leaving me there feeling stupid. I walked over to the booth and grabbed the phone.

"You gon' pick up the phone?"

She grabbed the phone and snapped on me.

"Why the fuck are you even up here, Jaw? You made the decision to step out on me. Now do you."

I knew I was wrong, but damn shawty wasn't playing fair.

"Who the fuck was ole boy?"

"My friend, Slim. Not that I owe you anything. We done nigga. I'll see you when I touch down." *Click!*

She hung up and walked off. When I walked out of the visiting room, the same C.O. winked at me and smiled. I mugged her ass. Ole thirsty ass hoe! I hurried up and got the hell up out of that building. As soon as I hit the car, I called Poohman.

"Yo, whud up, nigga? You in Wisconsin yet?"

"Man, why the fuck is it that when I just went up to the county trying to make shit right with that ole young dumb ass hoe, she had some other dude up there, Joe."

"Whoa, Ju? She getting down like that?"

"Change of plans, bruh. I'm chilling this weekend. Handle shit for me."

"I think you still need to take shawty's ass to la-la land. Don't let that shit that just happened cloud your judgment. Kill that bitch!"

"I'ma get up with you Monday."

ReRe

I was more than ready to go take care of Lil Man. Things had gone too far. If he didn't die soon, Ju was going to spend the rest of her life in jail. I wasn't leaving that house until I knew for sure that Lil Man was dead! New Year's Eve was going to be a bloody one. Where the fuck was Dirty's ass? I hit her line.

"Nigga, where the fuck are you? I'm outside the crib now."

"I'm looking right at you. Get out and walk through the lot."

It was cold as hell. Damn! I hopped out and threw my hood on. By the time I made it to her, she already had her gun out.

"You ready?"

"Yeah, but E what's the plan?"

She smiled and held up a gas can.

"Girl, what you 'bout to do with that?"

"I poured gasoline all around the windows and the base of the house. I'ma light the trail; and when the house go up in flames, I'm shooting everybody that run up outta there."

I doubled over laughing so hard that I farted! That was the funniest shit that I've heard in a long time.

"E, where do you come up with this shit?"

"It's gonna work, watch. You ready?"

"Yep. Let's see you pull this off, genius."

Lil Man

When I wasn't out trying to kill people, it was boring. Here I was sitting at home looking at T.V. JoJo was acting all standoffish as if I owed her something. She was probably mad because I ain't been home. Aww, I didn't know she cared.

"JoJo?"

She came out of the bedroom looking pissed.

"What?"

"What? What's the matter with you?"

"Nothing. What did you call me for?"

"Make me and KeeKee something to eat."

"What you want?"

"Some chicken wings and fries."

"Ain't no more fries."

"Then go to the store and get some."

"You gon' send me to the store in the cold?"

"Yeah, what's wrong with your feet? I been in the streets all week. I'm tired."

"You know what? Nothing."

Lazy ass bitch. I walked back to the couch and reached for the blunt that KeeKee had. I really didn't care for weed, but ever since he started lacing it with coke I been hooked!

"Aye, open a window. I'm hot as hell."

I hopped up and opened the window. A nice breeze came through. I got a whiff of nothing but gasoline.

"What the fuck?"

That ugly ass gremlin makes me sick. Lord, please don't let my baby come out looking like him. I had to go outside in the cold? Wait a minute. I grabbed my phone and called E.

"What up? You tell that nigga to leave?"

"Nope. I'm leaving."

"Hurry up and get out. I'm about to set the house on fire."

"WHAT?"

Shit, I screamed so loud that Lil Man came running.

"What's wrong with you?"

"Nothing. Mia just said something that I wasn't expecting."

He bought it because he walked back in to the living room.

"I'm leaving right now. Where your car at?"

"On Marquette."

Dirty E

I put my plan on hold just for a few seconds. Re's nosey ass peeped my hesitation.

"What you waiting for?"

"I'm waiting for JoJo to come out."

"Man, light that shit. I'm shooting whoever comes out, fire or not!"

"Re, she pregnant."

"It ain't yours. I'm gonna aim straight for her stomach. Fuck her and that bastard child."

Damn, that girl was special. I couldn't let her shoot JoJo. She was my problem.

"I'll handle JoJo. End of discussion."

Two minutes later, JoJo came out with a little extra pep in her step. I saw ReRe tighten her grip on her gun.

"Easy killa."

Show time! I ran across the street and lit the house on fire. *WHOOF* The flames wrapped around the house in seconds.

"Whoa, shit!"

I almost set my damn self on fire. When I made it back to Re, she was in her shooting position.

"Let's drop these fools, Re."

Lil Man

"Damn KeeKee, what's taking that hoe so long?"

"That's yo slow ass broad. Shit, it smell like something's already burning."

I sat up on the couch because I smelled it, too. I went to the window to look outside. *WHOOSH!*

"AW SHIT! THE HOUSE ON FIRE. COME ON JOE, WE GOTTA GO!"

I grabbed the front door knob and turned it. Thank God that it wasn't hot. As soon as KeeKee and I ran out of the house, all hell broke loose!

ReRe

I saw the front door fly open.

"Hell yeah."

I wasted no time letting my gun bust. *BOC, BOC, BOC, BOC* Damn, I was in love with the sound of gunfire.

Dirty E

I had just made it in position. I heard Re say, "Hell yeah." Then total chaos ensued. I saw Lil Man try to jump over the rail on the porch. I aimed at the other nigga and let my Tec speak. *TAT, TAT, TAT, TAT, TAT*

"Don't run now, nigga."

This was definitely a do or die situation. Here we were in

broad daylight trying to assassinate these niggas.

"ReRe, don't let that nigga get away!"

I took off running after the other nigga when Re called me "E, don't! The police are coming!"

I turned to my left and saw two squad cars coming in our direction.

"SHIT! Run, Re. Meet me at the spot."

I thought I was talking to Re, but that bitch broke out on me. I took off running through the alley and jumped a few gates to get to my car. JoJo was already in it. I jumped in and turned on the heat.

"Shit, I'm cold."

She was staring at me.

"Did you get him?"

"Shit, I don't know."

She put her head in her hands and rocked back and forth. I didn't wanna say shit but it was true. I don't think we hit either one of them niggas. Look, you know you can't go back home. That nigga is probably gon' figure this shit out."

TWENTY-FOUR

Chapter

Mia

The ride to Wisconsin was beautiful. There wasn't much snow in Chicago, but the further north we went the more snow we saw. I noticed that LJ was really quiet. He had barely said two words. I knew enough about men to know that if they wanted to tell you something they would. I reached for his hand and he grabbed mine.

"LJ, you a'ight, boo?"

"Yeah, why?"

"You've been quiet."

"I'm just thinking about what the new year is gon' bring."

I knew what I wanted for the New Year. When we finally got to the cabin, it was breathtaking. It looked like a frozen forest. Coming from the projects, I never had the opportunity to see something so pretty before. LJ just laughed.

"Damn, ma, you stuck?"

"Shut up. It's crazy out here. This is so pretty. I'ma 'bout to take a selfie."

The view was amazing, but when we stepped outta the car I took off running for the door. It was cold as shit.

"Aw hell naw. It's colder than that thang."

After we settled in, I asked LJ if he was hungry. I grabbed a few steaks out of the freezer and started the oven. LJ was on his phone, and I guess the conversation was an important one because he put on his coat and went on the porch. I looked around and took in the sights. A girl could get used to this type of treatment. I thought a lot about what JoJo had said to me. I was falling for this man, yet I barely knew anything about him. She was right. I didn't even have the other number to his phone. If I was the one that he was spending his time with, then I should have had all access granted. I heard his other phone ring, and I went to grab it but it had already stopped ringing. This was the phone that I didn't have the number to. I quickly called my phone; and when I heard my phone ring, I hung up and erased the outgoing call. As soon as I put his phone down, he came walking back in the door looking pissed.

"Boy, why is yo face all bawled up? We came here to relax. Turn them phones off, and let me cater to you."

He grabbed both of his phones and turned them off. After the food was done, we laid in front of the fireplace and ate. The conversation turned out better than I expected. Two hours later and three bottles of Merlot, it was now time to kick shit off.

"You ready for all of this. LJ?"

"Man, shawty, get naked!"

We fucked right there on the throw rug in front of the fireplace. This nigga's dick game was impeccable! I was falling hard for this man.

"Damn LJ, right there. Baby, yes it's that spot."

"You like this dick, huh?"

"Yes, baby, I love it."

"Then suck it!"

I jumped on my knees and got my Monica Lewinsky on. I

took all nine inches in my mouth and made that nigga's toes crack.

"Damn bitch, suck that shit. I'm 'bout to nut. You better swallow it all."

I was down to get freaky, but the way he was fucking my mouth I was a little concerned. I was so glad that he came. I wasn't glad that he held my head still with his hand and made me swallow his entire nut. He was a little bit too rough for me. I was going to have to talk to him about that later. I took my bag upstairs to run me a bath. *Beep* I heard my phone beeping indicating that I had a missed call.

"Damn, who called me?"

I walked my drunk ass over to the toilet and sat down after grabbing my phone. I almost threw up when I saw who had called me. The missed call was from Jaw. How the fuck did he get my number? Shit. Did he know who I was? I sat there trying to figure things out. My buzz was gone! I called the number back private twice. No answer. When I looked up, LJ was coming towards me. I tried to relax. I didn't want him to see me so rattled.

"Was that you that just called my phone and hung up?"

My head started spinning. That's when it all hit me.

"Oh my God!"

Jaw

After leaving the county, my head was all fucked up. I knew that I had crossed the line, but to see JuJu getting some attention from another dude hurt me. I was all inside my feelings. She changed my plans. I was going to bring Mia's scandalous ass up here to the cabin and freeze her body at the bottom of the lake. But after that scene at the county, I just wanted to chill, fuck her brains out, and then re-group. The drive to the cabin was quiet for me. My girl hit me below the belt. Shawty tried to make small talk, but I wasn't on that. She knew it, as well.

"LJ, you a'ight, boo?"

"Yeah, why?"

"You've been so quiet."

"Just thinking about what the new year is gon' bring."

I wasn't lying though. Ju's trial was days away. If she beat that case, where would that leave us? When we got to the cabin, I started the fire in the fireplace and got ready to relax. *ring ring* I checked the caller I.D.

It was Poohman. Even though I wasn't gon' kill the bitch; I still didn't want her in my business. I put on my coat and hit the porch.

"Whud up, bruh?"

"Man, shit always popping over East. Re and Dirty just made a move on Lil Man."

"What's the verdict?"

"Shit, they don't know. The police came and they got little, but um what's good? You gon' handle that other business?"

"Joe, I'm chilling. I don't know bruh."

"You better figure something out, because when Ju beats that case, the city is 'bout to have problems once she links up with them other two maniacs.

"Let me call you back later."

The rest of the night was cool. We got fucked up and I blew her back out. After I nutted in her mouth, I was satisfied. I dozed off for a minute. When she got up from next to me, I woke up. I didn't trust that bitch, so I was on to her every move. She went into the bathroom and ran a bath. I turned my phones back on so I could check my messages. My business phone rang. It was private. I chose not to answer it. The second time it rang; I glanced towards the bathroom and saw shawty on the phone. What the fuck was she doing? I jumped up with my phone in my hand and headed straight for the bathroom.

"Was that you that just called my phone private?"

She looked at me and said, "Oh my God."

I guess she had finally figured out that I knew her secret.

"Oh your God what?"

She backed away from me and grabbed her purse.

"What the fuck are you doing?"

That girl pulled her pistol on me and started crying.

"Why?"

I was stuck.

"You are the one pointing the gun at me. Fuck you asking me why for?"

"I didn't know. I mean it wasn't like that."

"Put that gun down before you accidently shoot me."

"Did you know who I was?"

"I been knew, but I wasn't gon' do shit to you."

I had to make it sound good. The bitch was pointing a big ass gun at me.

"I feel so stupid. I fell for you."

"Look, we can go home and part ways. If you shoot me, my peoples are gon' kill you because they know I brought you up here."

"LJ, why did you lie about your name?"

"I didn't lie about shit. What the fuck you think L3 stands for? LockJaw. You never even asked what LJ meant. Fuck all that, we leaving."

I took a chance and walked off as if I was in control. I prayed that she didn't shoot me in my back. Damn thinking with my dick.

I should have listened to Poohman. I just hope I can make it up outta here alive.

TWENTY-FIVE

Chapter

Ashley

My body was sore. My skin was raw and full of bruises. I felt so broken. As bad as I felt, I was so thankful that they found me. I had to be rushed to the hospital, because the urine and the feces gave me a real bad respiratory infection. I was just waking up when Boo and—oh my God—Lil Mama...! Boo was smiling from ear to ear.

"Hey hoe, you a'ight?"

"I'm feeling better now. Thank y'all for finding me. What made you even look for me, Boo?"

"Well, I did my own little investigation on this heffa Lil Mama and found out who helped her. I was calling you because I wanted to let you know what I found out. You hadn't returned none of my calls, so I got worried. Me and Heidi broke into Dirty and Tiki's crib to snoop through your shit."

I gave her a dirty look.

"Bitch, don't look at me like that. I was worried. Anyway, we almost got killed by some niggas that were trying to break in."

"Wait, what?"

"Girl, yes. We had to haul ass up outta there. We hit your crib next. I remembered you saying that you had him under your watch. I just figured that you had an address or something at your crib. It was a mess when we got there."

"Well? What y'all find?"

"A big ass dick in your nightstand."

All of us turned our heads to see Heidi standing there with a pink, yellow, and turquoise mink, with some badass Michael Kors thigh-high boots on.

"All right, bitch I see you."

Boo started shaking her head.

"Bitch, why you walk up in here looking like a peacock?"

"Fuck you, bitch. This shit is hot and you know it."

"So I see that you found Mandingo, huh?"

All of them turned their noses up at me. Boo, just put her head down.

"Anyway, we found an address and name in your nightstand. That's how we found you."

Lil Mama cleared her throat.

"I actually found you. I'm just saying…"

"Lil Mama, how did you find the house?"

"Before I had that accident, I was following his ass around. I wanted to reach out to y'all; but after all the shit we've been through, I should stay away. If I stayed in the shadows and killed him, then Ju would be all right. Together, we are all targets. Things are really about to heat up now since we missed our mark."

I closed my eyes because she was right. We were all at the mercy of that sick ass bastard.

"Y'all, he did some fucked up shit to me."

Boo grabbed my hand.

"Relax, baby. Ju's trial is in a few days. Just relax."

"What's the plan?"

"We got our lil gunners out there looking for Lil Man. If we can at least get him, then we might have a chance."

"Visiting hours are now over."

I didn't want them to leave.

"See y'all later."

Lil Mama stayed behind.

"What's good, Lil Mama?"

"I think I can hang that nigga on kidnapping."

"Who did he kidnap?"

"You and I got it on camera."

Lil Man

"Think about it, nigga. Yo bitch set us up!"

"Chill cuz, she wouldn't do that. She knows better."

"You send the bitch to the store, and three seconds later the house is on fire. When we run out, motha fuckers start shooting at us. I got shot in my fucking leg. I done already lost two brothers over your shit. My momma told me to never come back out West. This shit is all yo fault."

I was about to shoot that nigga in his mouth if he didn't shut the fuck up.

"DON'T CALL HER NO BITCH! Watch yo mouth. That's my baby mama, fool. Now as I said, she wouldn't do that. She loves me. I'll show you."

I picked up the phone and called her. I hoped that he was wrong. When I dialed her number, there was no answer. This was a fucked up way to bring in the New Year. But fuck it! At least I was alive ... for now.

157

ReRe

That was a close call. We're getting sloppy. I knew that I didn't hit Lil Man. I would have chased him if the police hadn't shown up. I just wanted to chill for New Year's Eve. I really needed to go see JuJu. I drove to Boo's crib to see if she would take me up there. *Knock, Knock*

"Who is it?"

"Boo, it's me, ReRe."

When the door opened, I almost fainted. It was one thing to hear that Lil Mama was alive, but to actually see her it was a bit much. She grabbed me by the arm.

"Don't just stand out there. It's cold as hell!"

I didn't know I was crying until she wiped my face. That lady was indeed like a mother to me. These last few months had been extremely hard on me. I was just so happy to see her.

"Lil Mama, I'm so glad that you are okay. You look great."

"Thank you baby. What brings you over here unannounced?"

"I was actually looking for Boo to see if she would take me up to the county to see JuJu."

"Don't tell her about me yet. I just don't want her to know yet."

I didn't understand that.

My bestie needed that type of good news.

"Um, well okay. I was definitely about to tell her."

"I wanna get that damn detective first before I show my face. I just want her to focus on her case. I'll be there."

We had too much shit going on. We haven't even been making money. Rule number one, you can't war and make money at the same time. The streets were hot in the middle of winter.

158

Boo came walking out of the kitchen with a cup of hot tea.

"Here lil girl. I know yo ass is cold. Any word on Lil Man?"

Damn! I hated to be put on the spot. I couldn't lie. I was too much of a G for that shit.

"Well, E and I just tried to kill him and some nigga today. We would have finished the job, but the police came, so I took off.

"Okay, listen, don't do shit else until after Ju's trial."

"But boo, if we don't kill Lil Man, he's going to testify against her."

"Lil Mama has something on Malone that could possibly send his ass away for the rest of his life. So just hold off on all that shoot 'em up bang bang shit. Okay?"

"Tell E it was her idea to set the house on fire and shoot whoever that came running out."

Boo and Lil Mama both fell out laughing. I hoped that all went well. I miss my girl. I needed her home with me. I could hold off on killing until then.

TWENTY-SIX

Chapter

Ju Ju

One week later

Today was the day my trial started. I had a long conversation with my lawyer and he told me that it could go either way. Boo came to see me before it was time for court and brought me a professional pants suit.

"Thank you, Boo. I wish my auntie was here."

"Don't worry. She's always going to be here with you. Just relax. We got this."

"We? I'm the one going on trial for a double murder. If I lose, I'm the one fucked. Not 'we.'"

"I understand your frustration, but lil girl, watch your mouth. I'm still your godmother. Respect me!"

"Have you heard from Jaw?"

"Yeah. He asked about you."

I wanted to tell her how triflin' her nephew was, but that was our business. I was going to handle that if I made it outta here.

"Tell him I love him, and I hope that he had fun. He'll know what I meant." The C.O. came and tapped on the door.

"Time's up!"

"I love you, Boo."

"I love you, too, baby. I'll be out there."

I didn't know how boring court actually was, until I sat there fighting to stay awake. The prosecutor was an ugly white man with a baldhead and cheap suit. He painted a very disturbing picture of me.

"Ladies and gentlemen of the jury, I stand before you today seeking justice for Shauntae Morgan and Tamiko St. Clair. They were both brutally murdered by that monster sitting right over there."

When he pointed at me, all eyes were on me. Let me tell you that shit made me wanna crawl up under the table. There was a member of the jury that had to be in her late 60's. She mugged me so hard that I had to look away. Not because she made me nervous, but because I didn't want to mug her old wrinkled ass back.

"I'm going to prove that Ja'ziya Campbell viciously attacked and murdered her best friend and legal guardian. Why? We'll never know. She needs to be convicted of double murder and put away. Forever!"

I turned to look at Boo and I was shocked to see Jaw sitting next to her. When our eyes locked, I wanted to cry. I felt sad because if I beat this, it was a chance that I was going to murder his black ass for breaking my heart. Dang, he looked good though. Punk ass nigga!

After that bullshit happened with Mia at the cabin, I had been on my solo shit. The ride back to the city was tense. She cried the whole ride back. I wasn't sure if she wanted me to feel sorry for her or what. I got so tired of all that sniffling and shit that I turned my radio up high on her ass. I discovered her little secret, and she couldn't say shit. When I pulled up to her crib, it looked as if somebody tried to burn it down. It was fucked up but it wasn't anything that couldn't be fixed.

"Can you help me with my bags?"

"Man, bitch you better get the fuck outta my car before I stomp yo fucking ears together."

I pulled off before she even closed the door. Stupid bitch! I spent the rest of my New Year's holiday alone. I hit the streets and put my mind back in grind mode. JuJu's trial was less than a week away. I needed to get my mind right if I was going to be there for her. Hopefully when she came home, we could go back to being Bonnie and Clyde.

The first day of her trial, I woke up feeling anxious. I didn't know what to expect. I called Poohman to see if he wanted to come with me.

"Bruh, I can't. It's cracking out here. Tell my lil sis to keep her head up."

"A'ight."

I got dressed and hit the streets. I couldn't help but think about what would happen if she didn't beat this case and come home. *Ring, Ring* I really didn't feel like being bothered. I looked at the screen and saw Mia's number.

"WHAT!"

"I think that we should talk now that things have cooled down."

"Shawty ain't shit to talk about. Everything about you was a lie. I fucked up with my girl and let yo bum ass in. I'm glad that you was on some other shit. Had I known sooner that you was Big Moe's cousin, I would have bodied yo ass."

"LJ didn't know until the night at the cabin that you were the same Jaw that played a part in all of my family's drama. I fell for you. I thought that we could build something. Now you're telling me it was all a mistake?"

"I love my girl and that's that. I ain't fucking with you. So if you're still planning on making any moves against me, you gon' fuck around and end up just like them pussy ass niggas you loved."

"Damn, I thought we had something special. That's how you speak to me?"

Was this chick serious?

"Man, Joe, miss me with all that shit. You were trying to have me killed. That shit sounds crazy. I let you suck my dick and now you are in love? You need to thank God that yo ass is still alive. We ain't got shit between us. And if you see me in the streets, bitch, you better act as if you don't know me.

"Nigga, you got me twisted. I wonder what yo bitch will say about me if she knew who I was."

"You can't threaten a nigga like me, hoe. She already knows about yo THAT ass. You thought you did something by answering my phone, but you didn't. I fucked up on my girl when I fucked yo ass. Yo pussy whack ass fuck. Get the fuck off my line hoe!" *Click*

That's what the fuck I get for fucking around. Now I had to worry about that psycho. As a matter of fact, no I didn't. I picked up my phone.

"What the hell you want, nigga?"

"Damn, shawty, that's how you answer the phone?"

"For you? Yeah."

"A'ight. Re, you got every reason to be upset. I fucked up big time. Now ole girl is threatening to do something to JuJu because I don't want her ass."

I had to make the shit sound good. If I would have just asked her to get at Mi, she would have cursed me out and some more shit.

"I should fuck yo ass up too for putting my girl in that position. Ole girl ain't gon' do shit to JuJu. She already on a countdown to death. I'ma get her ass."

"Where are you at right now?"

"On my way to court to support my girl."

"Me too. I'll see you there. We can sit together."

"No we can't, nigga. You done lost all cool points with me. I should pop yo ass anyway." *Click!*

On the real, I just might have to shoot Re's ass. Don't nobody put no fear in my heart. I ain't even gon' lie. That lil hoe does make me nervous. I found a parking spot and then hauled ass. I was late as shit. By the time I got in the courtroom, it had already started. I sat next to my auntie, Boo.

She grabbed my hand and held it.

"You're late."

"I know. I didn't know if I should show up with all the shit I've been putting her through."

"You know damn well you should be here, no matter what. That right there is your girl."

I think JuJu must have felt us talking about her because she turned around and looked dead at us. When our eyes locked, I saw so much anger, love, hurt, and pain in her eyes. I do know that if she does beat this case, I was going to have a big problem on my hands.

TWENTY-SEVEN

Chapter

Detective Malone

"I don't care what it takes. I want those bitches dead!"
I threw my phone across the room in frustration. My ass was going down if I didn't find those bitches that broke up in my house. Officer Dixon got lucky. I got a cleaning service to come out and clean my basement from top to bottom. I told them I had a few pit bulls that I was caring for. I needed to lay low if I wanted that little bitch convicted. I called Derrick because I needed him to go over a few things with me. *Ring, Ring*

I got up and grabbed my phone that I had just thrown. Speaking of the devil: "Where the hell have you been boy?"

"Some bad things have happened. Can I come stay with you until this trial shit is over?"

Aw hell no! I didn't want that damn, little street punk living under the same roof with me. But damn I needed him.

"Derrick, my home is a mess. How about I put you up in a room until after the trial is over?"

"You can do that. You gotta feed me, too. My pockets are on E, and I need some clothes to wear."

"Damn, is that all?"

"You got an extra car I could drive?"

"Yeah right? You better stick to stealing them."

I was getting too old for this shit. I should have quit while I was ahead. I just wanted some extra security before retirement. I mean, I couldn't travel the world on a yacht with my budget. I deserved more, and I intend to get what's owed to me.

I woke up this morning feeling like a new man. Today was the day that I appeared in court with Derrick. I was ready to be down with him for good. That little leech has been getting on my damn nerves, but I had to play nice. He was my whole case. After I nailed Ms. Ja'ziya Campbell with those double murders, I made the mayor very happy. I just have to see the case through and get my conviction. When court was over, I was leaving the city behind. Forty years of this shit was enough.

"Come on, Derrick. What the hell is taking so long?"

I knocked on his hotel door and heard nothing. I checked my watch and walked back to my car.

"Where the hell is that kid?"

I was worried. The prosecutor tore into my character like kids at Christmas opening presents. Fast! My lawyer was quick on his toes but first impressions were the most important.

"Do you think the jury bought that shit?"

"It's not really about what they bought. It's about who tells the better story."

"Well, after what that bald headed Uncle Tom said yesterday, we might be in trouble."

My lawyer looked like a square. He was black, 6'2". He was well dressed and talked immensely proper. No sense of street smarts, or so I thought. He leaned in to whisper to me.

"I see that you doubt me. I'm from the streets, too. Rockwell Gardens to be exact. Don't let the suit and these Urkel glasses fool you. We are in their world now. No matter how high we black folk climb on that ladder called success, we are still never good enough. We are always targets. The jury ain't just looking at you. They're looking at me, as well. I have to be proper, on point, and ready. I know what I'm doing. Let me do me, all right? Or should I use your lingo a'ight?"

"Right."

"Come on then. Let's go to war."

My lawyer showed his ass that day. He made the prosecutor look like a rookie. I mean he went over childhood drama to my good grades in school. Thank God I had good grades in school. The picture that he painted of me was better than a fancy Picasso was. It was a plus for us today. Tomorrow was going to be the real test. The state called its first and only witness Lil Man. When I got back to my cell, I was exhausted. I cried myself to sleep. If I didn't beat that case, I knew that I wasn't going to be able to do life in a place like this. I tried to think happy thoughts, but I couldn't. There was a dark cloud hanging over this building. I found myself dialing Jaw's number. Not because I wanted to talk, but because I just wanted to hear his voice.

"Yo? Why you calling my phone private?"

I missed him so much. Why did he have to mess everything up?

"Ju?"

I didn't realize that I had thought out loud.

"I hate you for messing everything up. Why didn't you just wait? Was that too hard?"

"Naw baby, it wasn't hard. I fucked up. Let me come see you

today?"

I didn't wanna see him. I just didn't think I was going to be able to handle that.

"I'm good. Wait 'til I beat my case. I don't need all the distractions."

"I'm here, ma, I love you."

I fought hard to keep my composure. I wanted to break down.

"We'll see." *Click!*

I hung up and decided to take a nap.

"Ju? Wake up. Wake yo ass up, girl."

I opened my eyes and couldn't believe what I was looking at.

"Tiki! Bitch, you dead. Don't be haunting my dreams; you know I'm scared of that type of shit."

She smiled and hit my leg.

"Get up and talk to me. I love you. You gon' beat this case. Focus on coming home."

"Coming home where?"

Even as a ghost, she still had a sense of humor.

"Not home with me dummy, unless..."

"Uh, hoe, I'm not ready to be with you."

"Don't let Lil Man get away with killing me."

I started to cry but she stopped me.

"Cut all that crybaby bullshit out. Just be ready. You'll get your chance."

She started to fade.

"Tiki? Don't go."

"JuJu, wake up!"

I jumped up and my cellie was standing there looking at me as if I was crazy.

"Bitch what? Stop staring at me."

"Well, quit talking in your sleep then. The C.O. just called you. I think you got a visitor."

I washed my face, brushed my teeth, and walked to the C.O's station.

"Campbell, you got a visitor."

I didn't feel like being bothered. Maybe Jaw came anyway. I was grateful that he came, but I really didn't wanna see him. I was escorted to the visiting building. I found a booth at the end of the room. I always chose that booth because I didn't want nobody in my business in case I cried. Five minutes passed and no Jaw.

"What the fuck, man?"

I was about to get up when this chick walked up to the booth. I didn't know her so I didn't pick up the phone. She sat down anyway and pointed to the phone. Maybe she had the wrong booth. She sat there looking at me. Now I was curious. I picked up the phone and wasted no time getting straight to the point.

"Do I know you?"

She licked her lips and smiled. Okayyyy.

"No you don't know me, but you should know that he loves me."

Huh? Who was this bitch?

"Excuse me? Who the fuck are you?"

"I'm the bitch that replaced you. Jaw wants to be with me, so quit calling him. If you do get out, you better stay away from my man. If I catch you, there's gonna be problems."

I had to stand up and take a step back to size that hoe up. She was so lucky that the glass was bulletproof.

"So let me get this straight. You came all the way up here to the county jail to tell me that? Bitch, you better hope and pray that I don't beat this case; because if I do, where the fuck are you going to hide?"

"Lil girl, you must not know about me or who my family is."

"Bitch, fuck you and yo family. I'ma make sure you see me. This ain't what you want. You better ask your cousin and your brothers. Aw wait, you can't, but fucking with me you'll see 'em real soon."

I hung up and gave that bitch my back as I walked outta the room. I couldn't wait to get out. That bitch was definitely going to see me!

TWENTY-EIGHT

Chapter

Mia

I didn't appreciate how that pussy ass nigga played me. You might think I played myself, but for real, y'all, how the fuck was I supposed to know that LJ and Jaw were the same person? I'm gonna fuck my shady ass sister up because I bet my life that she knew. Why didn't she tell me? I'm gonna get her ass. After I got back from that cabin, I threw myself back into hustling. I had to move because it looked as if somebody tried to bomb my damn house. I haven't even seen JoJo or heard from her. That shit made me really suspicious, because she didn't have anywhere else to go. I needed to find out Jaw's bitch's real name. I was going to make my way up to the county and have a little chat with her. She needed to know who I was, because Jaw and I were going to be together. He was mad, but he was going to have to get over that shit in order for us to be together. We were going to be together. Period! Where the fuck was my phone? *Ring, Ring* I checked the screen and saw that it was Lil Man.

"What the hell you want, maniac?"

"I think your sister tried to have me killed."

"Why do you say that?"

"I told her to go to the store, and when she left I smelled

gasoline. When I looked out the window, the crib went up in flames. My cousin and me jumped up and ran out of the house. As soon as we hit the porch, somebody started shooting at us. We got away, but ever since then I ain't heard from her."

I knew how I was gonna get her ass back.

"Damn, lil bro, that's fucked up if she did that. I'm glad you're okay. I knew that she was grimy but never did I think that she would try and have the father of her baby killed."

I had to lay it on thick because I needed him. He was a killer.

"Mia, how could she? I loved her and my baby. Where is she at?"

"I don't know. I haven't heard from her. Where are you at?"

"I've been in this hotel room. I'm supposed to testify against JuJu in a few days."

"What's her real name?"

"Ja'ziya Campbell. Why?"

"I got some unfinished business with her, that's all."

"To be honest with you Mia, I don't wanna testify against her. I wanna kill her and the rest of her little clique."

"Well I don't know about all that snitching. Where I come from we hold court in the streets."

"But that detective dude want me..."

"Is he paying you?"

"Nope!"

"Then fuck dude. Let him solve his own case. I'm 'bout to hit the county.

"Her visiting days ain't 'til tomorrow."

I was about to ask him how he knew, but I thought better of it.

"You want me to come get you?"

"Yeah. Fuck the courts. I'ma kill 'em all!"

"Where you at?"

The next day

After putting Lil Man up, I hit the streets to collect my money. Tomorrow he was supposed to testify in court. If he didn't show, he said that the detective dude was going to come after him because he knew too much. I told him that I wouldn't let shit happen to him. What? He didn't need to know that I was lying. As soon as I found JoJo, I was going to let Lil Man get her ass. Blood ain't thicker than water. She showed me that. So fuck her and that demon child that she's carrying. I checked my watch. It was shift change at the county. By the time I made it up there, it wasn't that crowded. Thank goodness. I didn't want to risk running into Jaw or any of her other little friends. When I walked in, I saw her sitting at the last booth on the end. I had to admit, she was cute. She looked like she didn't have a care in the world. I was kind of jealous. I see what Jaw saw in her. I picked up the phone and waited for her to do the same. After staring at me for a few seconds, she finally picked the phone up.

"Do I know you?"

I licked my lips and smiled. I had to be extra. It was time to let this lil girl know that she was indeed being replaced.

"No you don't know me, but you should know that he loves me."

I was fucking with her head some. I could tell that I had her attention because she had a dumb ass look on her face.

"Excuse me? Who the fuck are you?"

"I'm the bitch that replaced you. Jaw wants to be with me, so quit calling him. If you get out, you better stay away from my man. If I catch you, there's gonna be problems."

She stood up and looked me up and down.

173

"So let me get this straight. You came all the way up here to the county jail to tell me that? Bitch, you better hope and pray that I don't beat this case; because if I do, where the fuck are you going to hide?"

We went back and forth for a while before she hung up and walked off. She had the balls to throw my cousin and my brothers being dead in my face. Hell yeah, I was going to enjoy taking her life. Jaw was mine!

TWENTY-NINE

Chapter

Detective Malone

I was fucked! Damn, that little shit Derrick. Today was the day that I was supposed to bring him to testify at court. He bailed on me. There goes my career. The mayor was going to have a field day over this case if she wasn't convicted. I made it to the courtroom before court started. I needed to speak with the prosecutor. I found him in the restroom.

"Um, Mark? I need to speak to you like now!"

"Malone, good day buddy. Where is Derrick?"

"I, um, can't find him."

"WHAT?"

"I need more time."

"We don't have more time damn it. I need him on the stand today."

"He's gone. You can use me, can't you? I can..."

"You can't do shit! Without that boy, all of this will be for nothing. I'm going to lose my job. They're going to demote me to the court's clerk. You've ruined my career."

"What about the jury?"

"What about 'em?"

"Money talks."

"Do you know what you're saying? If that gets out, we won't have a career. We'll share a jail cell. I'm telling you now, if one of them rats us out, I'm telling on your ass, too!"

"How much?"

"Give me $10,000. We can split it with like three jurors. It's three college students on the panel. I'm sure they could use it. You better hope this works."

To my surprise, all three of the college students took the money. Maybe there was a God.

JuJu

I didn't even bother to call Jaw and curse his dumb ass out. It was his fault that she was even able to get close to me. She definitely hit a nerve. I called ReRe and told her what happened.

"I'm going to ruin that nigga, Re."

"That shit is crazy. He called me a few days ago, and told me that I had the green light to get at her. That let me know that he ain't been fucking with her no more."

"The girl was serious when she came up here. In her mind, Jaw is hers. Do you think they fucked?"

"Don't think about that shit. I know for a fact that he loves the hell out of you. Yeah, he fucked up, but he's our family. We look out for family."

"I'm telling you, if I make it outta here I'm going to destroy this city until I find that bitch. Today, Lil Man is supposed to testify. I'm scared, Re."

"I know. Just pray. We ain't seen him around lately. E has been playing hostess to that little bitch, JoJo. She can't go back home. I guess Lil Man figured out that she set him up."

"That's crazy."

"Naw, the crazy part is that she's pregnant."

"It ain't E's!"

We started laughing our asses off.

"Damn, Re. She gave Lil Man some pussy? Yuk! They are calling me in for court. Where you at?"

"In front of the court building. I'll see you in there. Love you.''

"Okay, love you, too."

I was scared. I said a small prayer. I wished that my auntie were alive. I needed her to be here with me.

"Damn, auntie Lil Mama, I miss you so much."

When I got in the courtroom I saw Re, Poohman, and him. He looked at me and winked. I couldn't help but smile. I had so many mixed emotions, but now wasn't the time to figure them out.

"Everyone please rise. Court is now in session."

The prosecutor wasted no time calling its first witness: Detective Malone. He walked his fat ass in the courtroom. He seemed so sure of himself. Ole dirty motha fucker...

Boo

I had something for that detective if he thought that he was going to pin that shit on my goddaughter. Today was going to make or break the case. JuJu's lawyer had the evidence that was needed to damage the testimony of the detective. I watched Ashley's kidnapping tape myself. His ass was seen on tape, clear as day, dragging that girl out of his car and into his house. Lil Mama decided not to show her face at court today. I wondered when she was going to tell JuJu that she was alive. Ashley was making progress. She secretly filed charges against her boss. The precinct where they worked also had a copy of the kidnapping tape. It was only a matter of time before he too had his day in court. I stopped by Dirty's house to pick her up. *Knock, Knock* When the door opened, I wasn't expecting to see JoJo. I look at her little bump in her stomach and couldn't hold my tongue.

"I know that ain't E's baby, is it?"

"No ma'am, it's not. Come in."

I came in and looked around. She was definitely staying here.

"Where's E?"

"In the shower. Want me..."

"No thank you. I'll go get her."

I walked to the bathroom and opened the door. She was so into singing her song that she never heard me enter the room until I flushed the toilet.

"Aww, JoJo, what the fuck?"

She snatched the shower curtain open, saw me, and screamed.

"UGH! Boo, you scared the shit out of me."

"Un huh. What the fuck you got going on up in here?"

"It's a long story, but to make it short I kinda put her in danger."

"Um. I thought that you was supposed to..."

"I was, but the next time I saw her she was pregnant. I'ma goon, Boo, but I'm not a monster."

I felt where she was coming from.

"Well, E she can't stay here forever. If Lil Man finds out that she's here, it's going to be a problem."

"Don't worry. I'm on my shit. Let me get dressed so we can go."

"One more thing."

"Naw man, that ain't my baby."

THIRTY

Chapter

Young Meech

I've been handling a lot of my auntie's affairs. I was glad that Lil Mama showed her face. I was tired of playing Suzie the homemaker. My pockets suffered a little. My mind hasn't been right since I lost my three favorite girls. Boo and Lil Mama have been in my corner throughout the whole ordeal. I needed that. I had some big shoes to fill. I loved Re and Dirty, but I needed my own squad. It was time to show Chicago that King Meech lived on through me! I didn't want to get down with too many niggas. All I wanted was three people.

I needed an enforcer, someone who wouldn't hesitate to murk a nigga. I needed my left- and right-hand men. I knew just who to call. *Ring, Ring*

"Hello?"

"Heidi, this is Meech."

"Hey baby, how are you?"

"I'm good. Is Money Man and Outlaw around?"

"Money Man in his room with his lil girlfriend. You want me to get him?"

"Just tell him I'm about to slide on him."

"Um, Meech?"

"Yeah?"

"Money Man don't like you."

I laughed so hard I almost cried. That lady had no filters! She said whatever the fuck she wanted.

"It was all a misunderstanding. I'm sure we gon' be a'ight. Just tell him I'll be there in 30 minutes."

"You can tell him. Money Man, phone. If he curse yo ass out, I warned you. Be good baby."

"Who dis?'

"Whud up, this Young Meech. I'm 'bout to come holla at you. I got a business proposition for you and Outlaw."

"Man, dude, you upped a banger on me. We ain't got shit to talk about unless you tryin' to let me get that fade."

"Nigga you knew why I did that. It wasn't personal. You wanna fight? A'ight I'm on my way."

20 minutes later

I rung Heidi's bell ready for whatever. I knew that it was a good chance that I was gonna get jumped, but him and whoever was gonna have to work for that ass whooping. When Heidi opened the door, Money Man, Outlaw, and Money Man's girlfriend were all standing there ready. I had to laugh because they were dead ass serious. Now all I had to do was keep 'em from jumping me. I even left my gun in the car. Staring at them, I knew that I had made a good choice with choosing then.

"Come on in, baby."

I walked in and just got straight to the point.

"I want y'all to get money with me. Money Man, you got heart, and I need that in my line of business. Outlaw, I need you because I know that you won't hesitate to buss yo gun."

I had to butter the lil nigga up. When he gave me a side grin, I knew I had him.

"What about me?"

I turned to look at Money Man's girl. She had her hands on her hip, with her head tilted to the side.

"What about you? What can you do?"

"I know how to buss my gun, too. Whatever Money Man tells me to do, it gets done."

She could come in handy. I mean they could be Bonnie and Clyde or Ike and Tina. I really didn't give a fuck, as long as we made money. Money Man finally spoke up.

"Aside from that bullshit that happened. I would be willing to get down with you. You cool as shit, but don't ever pull another gun on me."

I let him speak his peace.

"I heard stories about yo father. I ain't no dick rider, but he was that nigga. It's a gang of money to be made, so let's get it. My girl got people in Indiana and Iowa, so when we ready we can expand."

See I knew that I was on to something with this group.

"Then it's official. I got another guy I want y'all to meet. He's not your average hustler, but he gets doe and he is book smart.'

Outlaw cleared his throat.

"Whud up, shawty?"

"We need a name. How about the Young Money crew?"

"Lil Wayne already got that name. We ain't no biters. Come up with something better."

After a little deliberation, the Chi City Boys were born.

THIRTY-ONE

Chapter

Ju Ju

W hen that fat ass detective got up on the stand, I held my breath. You must understand that there is some dirty ass cops out there that will do any and everything to get a conviction. I mean, he held me illegally at the station for hours without my guardian present. I scanned the courtroom looking for Lil Man. I locked eyes with Jaw. He whispered, "I love you." I just closed my eyes and tried to focus on the voice of my lawyer.

"So Detective Malone, you said that you received a tip from Crime Stoppers?"

"Yes, I did."

"What was said?"

Clearing his throat

"Well the caller told me that he knew who was responsible for the double murders that occurred on 88th and Marquette."

"I thought that Crime Stoppers' tips were mostly anonymous?"

"Oh, well, that person decided to give his name."

"Oh, okay. Let me ask you this. If I asked a few of your co-workers to describe what kind of person you are, they would say what?"

"Objection, your honor. Personal opinions are irrelevant."

"Your honor, I'm trying to establish how good or bad the credibility of this witness is."

"Overruled!"

"Detective Malone, please answer the question."

"Well, um, they would say that I'm a hard worker, persistent and reliable. Hell, I could go on for days. What's your point?"

"Who is Ashley Dixon?"

That question made him uncomfortable, because he started shifting around in his seat.

"She's an officer under my command, why?"

"She disappeared into thin air a few weeks ago. Do you know anything about that?"

The prosecutor flew out of his seat.

"Objection, your honor. What does that question have to do with this murder trial?"

My lawyer was treading on thin ice, because I could see that the judge was starting to get irritated.

"Counsel, what's the reason for all this?"

"I could prove that he has no business up here testifying against my client. His credibility is worthless. I would like to introduce Exhibit A, your honor."

The judge pointed his finger at my lawyer.

"This better be good."

I didn't know what was happening, but I had a feelings things were about to work out in my favor. While the court clerk was preparing the DVD, you could have heard a rat piss on cotton. It was that quiet. The screen went black, and then a house popped up.

"Detective Malone, who's house is that?"

"Th ... th ... that's my house. What is all this, counsel?"

My lawyer didn't say a word. He just pressed play. Thirty seconds into the tape, all hell broke loose. Everyone in the courtroom gasped. On the tape, you could see, clear as day, Detective Malone dragging a kicking and screaming Ashley by her hair. He punched her, and then pulled his gun out and pointed it at her. She put her hands up surrendering. He then put the gun back in the holster; and without warning, he punched her so hard in her face that he knocked her out cold. Damn, was all I could say to myself. The video went blank. The courtroom erupted in chaos. *BANG, BANG, BANG*

"Order in the court room." *BANG, BANG, BANG*

"Order, damn it. One more outburst and I'm clearing this courtroom out."

Detective Malone was caught red-handed. My lawyer looked at the jury and smiled.

"Ladies and gentlemen of the jury, you have just witnessed the state's star witness commit a very heinous crime. He also happens to be an officer of the law sworn to protect and serve the people. Yet he sits on this stand trying to play a part in convicting my client of a crime that she didn't commit."

I looked at the prosecutor and he looked as pale as a ghost. The judge looked at Malone with pure rage in his eyes.

"Detective, do you have anything to say?"

"I ... I ... I don't know what that is your honor."

"It looks like a kidnapping to me. Bailiff, escort his ass upstairs to booking, where he is to be charged with kidnapping and assault on Officer Ashley Dixon." *Bang*

It took three officers to take him up out of the courtroom. When I looked at the jury to see their reaction, I zoomed in on three white girls. They appeared mortified. They kept whispering back and forth with each other and shaking their heads. I called

my lawyer over and told him what I saw.
  "I'll check it out at recess."

THIRTY-TWO

Chapter

Lil Man

Instead of testifying against JuJu, I decided to hold court in the streets. I enjoyed role-playing. I was going to be the judge and the jury. In my eyes, all of their asses were guilty! I still haven't heard from JoJo. That made me want to hate her ass even more. I want my baby. I needed to find her. I knew that Mia was only being nice to me because she was mad at JoJo. You can't manipulate a manipulator. I planned on killing her ass anyway. I know she was calling Jaw and giving him information on me. I bought a tape recorder when I first moved in with them, because I already felt as if I couldn't trust 'em. I taped it under the living room table. I know everything they talked about. I wasn't tripping on JoJo telling Mia about my plans. I was pissed because they planned on getting me out of the way. That bitch, JoJo, is foul.

She really wanted me dead. The father of her baby. I'ma change all of that. After she had my baby, I was going to torture her to death. She was going to die a painful and slow death. I put that on my mama! That went for everybody. Anybody who plotted against me was going to feel me in a bad way. After I killed everybody, my baby and I were going to disappear for a while. I was outnumbered and out gunned. I hit up JoJo just to see if she would answer. When she finally did, I let her ass have it.

"Yes, Derrick."

"Why the fuck you ain't been answering the phone? Why you try and have me killed?"

"Um, you tripping. I just bought a charger and I..."

"BITCH, DON'T LIE TO ME! You have been lying. You and that whore sister of yours have been plotting on me for a while. I recorded you, bitch!"

I knew I had her then because she was quiet.

"I just wanna be done with all this killing shit. I want my baby to have a normal life, Derrick."

"You are tired of the killing? You ain't the one doing it, so why the fuck should you care? You thought that killing the father of your child was going to make things better?"

"You've gone too far."

"Those bitches are responsible for killing my whole family, and I'm the one who's gone too far?"

"But you started..."

I couldn't believe that bitch. Any feelings that I had for her just went out of the window. She was now a target like the rest of them hoes.

"Man, Joe, the only thing saving you is my baby."

"Yeah, and you'll never see it."

"I'm gonna make sure you suffer, bitch."

"Find me first, you pussy ass nigga." *Click!*

"Hello?" I needed to find her ass before she skipped town on me. She was a dead bitch walking. Mia was, as well!

I almost shit on myself when the judge allowed the tape to be played. It was hard to watch, but the judge needed to see it. Lil Mama did that. Ashley was mad as hell when Lil Mama first told her about the tape. She felt as if Lil Mama should have said something. Lil Mama told her that she was coming to get her but she had that accident. She also told her that Malone needed her. Lil Mama didn't think that he would go that far and do all that shit to her. With his ass finally out of the way and Lil Man as a no-show, we had this case in the bag. I pulled Ju's lawyer to the side to see what he thought about the recent turn of events.

"Hey Maria, how are you?"

"Fine. Tell me how things are looking now after that little circus."

He grabbed me by the arm and led me to the hallway.

"I can't say for sure, but I think the jury—well not all, but some—have been compromised."

"Compromised! How?"

"I'm almost sure that the detective and prosecutor paid some of them. It is sad to say but I've seen this a few times. I just have to prove it."

Those dirty motha fuckers. You see that's how they do us. They're scared to fight us in the courtroom the right way. The government is so corrupt. They always try to trick us or break the law to have their way.

"So how are you going to handle the situation?"

"Well, once I question them I'll go from there. I could smell deceit a mile away. I got this."

"How many do you think were compromised?"

"Three."

"I guess one of the jurors had a change of heart after I played the tape. Before you approached me, I was talking to her. She told me ... Wait, I can't tell you. Let me do my job. I wouldn't want blurting this out and possibly ruining your niece's chance of getting this dismissed."

I was so happy that I couldn't contain myself. I wasn't gonna tell Ju, but I broke my neck to get back in the courtroom to tell Heidi, Jaw, and her besties. Jaw damn near cried; he was so happy.

"That was some hoe ass shit, auntie. Oh well, at least she coming home now."

I looked at JuJu and saw her watching us. I smiled and waved. She returned the gesture. But when she looked at Jaw, I saw a lot of pain, hurt, and anger. Oooh wee. I hated to be him if she did come home.

Recess took forever. My lawyer was back and forth from the judge's chamber to the courtroom. The prosecutor looked as if he was about to have a heart attack. I kept looking at the three white girls on the jury panel. They gave me no eye contact. Finally, after about two hours, the judge came back in the room.

"All rise."

After the judge took his seat, he went the fuck off.

"I don't appreciate that my courtroom was used today as a circus."

He turned to the prosecutor.

"Please rise. It has been brought to my attention that you and Detective Malone paid three jurors to vote guilty no matter what."

"Your honor, that's absurd. I take my job very seriously."

"If that was the case, you would have never put that witness on the stand without doing your own investigation into his background. Had you done that, you would have known that he was under investigation by Internal Affairs for corruption,

189

extortion, and kidnapping. Where was the other witness?"

"I'm not sure. I need a few more..."

"Excuse my French, but I'm not giving you shit. You have wasted my time and the time of the courts. You have also committed a federal offense by trying to buy my jurors."

"But your honor..."

"Shut up! I hold you in contempt of court. You will be charged for your actions. It is prosecutors like you that make the justice system look bad. Bailiff? Get his ass outta my court room."

I was shocked. My judge was a G! He then turned to the jury panel.

"And as far the three jurors who decided that $3,000 a piece was worth sending someone to jail possibly for life for a crime that they may not have committed, you can forget about your next few semesters at school. Bailiff? Lock their asses up, as well!"

Okay. He let their asses have it. Where did that leave me? *Throat Clearing*

"Ms. Campbell pleases stand."

Aw shit! I had to hold on to my lawyer because I was so scared.

"I don't even know how to address you, young lady. I can't say that you are innocent, and I can't say that you are guilty. I read up on your background, and I commend you for going to school and getting good grades."

"Thank you, sir."

"I'm no fool, young lady. I know that you are not an angel. If you were, you would have never made it on Detective Malone's radar. I understand that you knew the victims?"

"Yes, sir. Tamiko was my best friend and Tae was my auntie."

"I'm sorry for your loss. The justice system is not all messed up like people think. However, today just showed me—and everyone else—that there are a few rotten apples in every bunch. You are very lucky, young lady. The state failed to prove that you were responsible for those murders. I hereby declare a mistrial. Ms. Campbell, you are free to go." *Bang, Bang*

I turned around and smiled at my family. Boo stood up.

"I'll be downstairs waiting for you."

"Okay."

When Jaw smiled at me, I kept a straight face. I didn't know how I was going to deal with him.

THIRTY-THREE |

Chapter

Mia

I was bored as hell sitting in the house. I was channel surfing when I turned to the midday news. My whole world came crashing down.

"In other news, charges were dropped this afternoon for the murder suspect who was accused of killing Tamiko St. Clair and Shauntae Morgan on Thanksgiving night. No statement was given by the D.A.'s office on why the charges were dropped. Stay tuned for the weather." Click

I shut the T.V. off and threw the remote.

"BITCH!"

It was wartime. Jaw was mine. That bitch had better watch her back!

Ju Ju

I made it back to the deck before dinnertime. I gave all my shit to my homie Jade. I was in my room on the phone about to make a call when my room door came open. I thought it was Jade.

"Bitch, you can have this phone, too."

I heard a familiar voice behind me, but it wasn't Jade.

"Lucky bitch! You thought I forgot about that shit, huh?"

When I turned around, I saw the same three hoes that I fought when I first got here. They were all standing in my little ass cell looking as if they were ready to do some damage.

"You still on that? Get the fuck away from me with all that bullshit."

I wasn't scared, but I had a bad feeling about this one. I jumped out of my bunk and tried to move towards the door. The ringleader pulled out a big ass shiny metal knife and lunged at me. I moved out of the way and pushed passed them other two bitches. I knocked them down and was almost at the door when I felt a burning sensation coming from my back.

"UGGHHH!"

"SHUT UP, BITCH!"

She stabbed me about three more times before I blacked out. When I came to, I heard Jade screaming.

"C.O., I NEED HELP! Ju ... stay with me, boo. You gon' be okay."

I was coughing up blood, so she turned me on my side. She grabbed a towel and wiped my face.

"Hold on, boo! Help is coming. C.O., I NEED MEDICAL, PLEASE, DAMN IT!"

I was starting to get colder and colder by the second. My whole life flashed before my eyes. I saw my mother come to me with open arms. She seemed so happy. I coughed and more blood came up.

"Ju, stay with me, please. They're coming."

I saw Jaw's face. He was holding my hand telling me how much he loved me. I was feeling myself getting weaker. *WHACK!* Jade slapped the shit out of me.

193

"Bitch, stop closing your eyes. We're gonna fight this shit."

How come I didn't see this coming? I didn't wanna go like this. I was only 16 years old, but I had been fighting all my life. I fought to be loved. I fought for respect. I fought for everything. Shit, I was tired. Now was the time that I really needed to fight. I didn't think I had it in me no more. I was starting to feel light-headed. What a fucked-up way to go.

"Damn, Lil Mama, they still take forever to process motha fuckers?"

"Shit, you should know. I ain't never been to the county."

I brought her to surprise JuJu. I left Jaw's ass at home. I didn't need her getting out, just turning around and going back in there for murder. This time she was going down. Two hours later and still no JuJu. Lil Mama jumped her ass outta the car and did her famous fuck-strut inside the lobby area.

I hurried up and caught up with her because her temper was going to land her ass in one of those jail cells upstairs. I didn't need JuJu coming out and her going in. By the time I made it in the building, she was already going off.

"It don't take no damn six hours to process one motha fucker. What the fuck is the hold up?"

I could tell that there was about to be some shit because the receptionist behind the desk looked like one of them ole project ass hood rat bitches. She eye-fucked Lil Mama before she went off.

"First off, don't be coming up in here like I owe you something. She'll be out when they are done processing her.

What's the name?"

"Ja'ziya Campbell."

She picked up the phone and made a call. The color drained out of her face causing my heart rate to speed up. Something was wrong. Lil Mama felt it too, because she started breathing really hard trying to calm down and catch her breath. The lady came from behind the desk and walked up to us.

"They said that the jail is on lockdown."

"Why?"

"Um, somebody was stabbed. I think it was the girl you looking for."

"Think or know? Don't play with me lil girl."

She looked around and stepped closer.

"I could lose my job for this. It is her."

"Lil Mama don't..."

It was too late. She snapped!

"FUCK!"

She hit the vending machine shattering the glass.

"She's just a fucking baby! Damn it."

I had to take control.

"I gotta go. Y'all have to leave. Call up here and ask for Captain Holmes."

I grabbed Lil Mama and we left.

"Calm down. Let me see what's going on."

As soon as we stepped outside, my phone rang. It was the same number that Ju had been calling me from.

"Hello, Ju?"

"No it's Jade. I'm her friend."

"Well is she okay?"

"Um, no. She was stabbed four times. She lost a lot of blood."

"Who did it?"

"Some hoes she got into it with. I was in the shower and they ran up in her room."

"Keep me posted, okay?"

"She told me to tell Jaw that she loved him."

"I'll deliver the message."

Mia

I prayed that my plan worked. There was no way that I was going to share him with her. *Ring, Ring*

"Hello?"

"You have a collect call from Marquisha Brown. Press 5 to accept."

"Whud up, cuzo? You got something for me?"

"Girl, shit been crazy up in here. Some lil bitch just got stabbed like four times. They just wheeled her ass up outta here on a stretcher."

"Damn, that's fucked up. Did she die?"

"She lost a lot of blood. When they found her, she ain't have a pulse."

"I'ma send you some money. Love you."

"Love you, too."

Now that's what the fuck I'm talking about. I got family everywhere it matters. If I couldn't have Jaw, he wouldn't have her. I called his phone.

"Yo? Why you keep calling me?"

"Damn, is that how you talk to your future wife?"

"My future what? Bitch, you crazy. My wife is JuJu. Get a life."

"Speaking of lives, at least I have mine."

"What the fuck is that supposed to mean?"
"Turn to the news."

Jaw

Man it was taking forever for Boo to bring my shawty back to me. Six hours and counting. I was starting to get impatient. What the fuck was she going to say to me? Better yet, what was she going to do to me? I was nervous.

My girl was crazy. *Ring, Ring*

I jumped up and grabbed my phone thinking it was Boo.

It was that hoe, Mia. We went back and forth for a few seconds. I wasn't about to argue with that bitch. I was about to hang up until she told me to turn to the news. I turned to channel 7 and listened.

"Breaking news. I'm Laura Lovespell reporting live from Channel 7 News. There has been a vicious stabbing at the county jail on 26th and California tonight. The jail was put on lockdown after an inmate preparing to go home was viciously stabbed four times. The inmate was airlifted to Holy Christ Hospital in critical condition. The inmate's name will not be released at this time. I will be following this tragic story. Brian ... back to you."

I sat there stuck. I know that wasn't about my baby. I heard Mia laughing on the phone.

"Hello? Jaw, are you there? See, if I can't have you, you won't have her."

"BITCH, I'MA KILL YOU!"

"Not if I don't kill you first."

My Besties PT 4

Revenge Is Mine

Coming Soon

Please support this author by leaving your review.

Thank You!

BOOKS BY GOOD2GO AUTHORS

GOOD 2 GO FILMS PRESENTS

THE HAND I WAS DEALT- FREE WEB SERIES
NOW AVAILABLE ON YOUTUBE!
YOUTUBE.COM/SILKWHITE212

To order books, please fill out the order form below:

To order films please go to www.good2gofilms.com

Name:_____

Address:_____

City:_____ State:_____ Zip Code:_____

Phone:_____

Email:_____

Method of Payment: Check   VISA   MASTERCARD

Credit Card#:_____

Name as it appears on card:_____

Signature:_____

Item Name	Price	Qty	Amount
48 Hours to Die – Silk White	$14.99		
Business Is Business – Silk White	$14.99		
Business Is Business 2 – Silk White	$14.99		
Childhood Sweethearts – Jacob Spears	$14.99		
Flipping Numbers – Ernest Morris	$14.99		
Flipping Numbers 2 – Ernest Morris	$14.99		
He Loves Me, He Loves You Not - Mychea	$14.99		
He Loves Me, He Loves You Not 2 - Mychea	$14.99		
He Loves Me, He Loves You Not 3 - Mychea	$14.99		
He Loves Me, He Loves You Not 4 – Mychea	$14.99		
He Loves Me, He Loves You Not 5 – Mychea	$14.99		
Lost and Turned Out – Ernest Morris	$14.99		
Married To Da Streets – Silk White	$14.99		
My Besties – Asia Hill	$14.99		
My Besties 2 – Asia Hill	$14.99		
My Besties 3 – Asia Hill	$14.99		
My Boyfriend's Wife - Mychea	$14.99		
My Boyfriend's Wife 2 – Mychea	$14.99		
Never Be The Same – Silk White	$14.99		
Stranded – Silk White	$14.99		
Slumped – Jason Brent	$14.99		
Tears of a Hustler - Silk White	$14.99		
Tears of a Hustler 2 - Silk White	$14.99		
Tears of a Hustler 3 - Silk White	$14.99		
Tears of a Hustler 4- Silk White	$14.99		
Tears of a Hustler 5 – Silk White	$14.99		
Tears of a Hustler 6 – Silk White	$14.99		
The Panty Ripper - Reality Way	$14.99		
The Panty Ripper 3 – Reality Way	$14.99		

Continued on next page.....

The Teflon Queen – Silk White	$14.99		
The Teflon Queen 2 – Silk White	$14.99		
The Teflon Queen 3 – Silk White	$14.99		
The Teflon Queen 4 – Silk White	$14.99		
The Teflon Queen 5 – Silk White	$14.99		
Time Is Money - Silk White	$14.99		
Young Goonz – Reality Way	$14.99		
Subtotal:			
Tax:			
Shipping (Free) U.S. Media Mail:			
Total:			

Make Checks Payable To:
Good2Go Publishing
7311 W Glass Lane,
Laveen, AZ 85339